SUMMER SOLSTICE

By

David H. Huffman

© 2002 by David Huffman. All rights reserved.

No part of this book may be reproduced, stored in a retrieval system, or transmitted by any means, electronic, mechanical, photocopying, recording, or otherwise, without written permission from the author.

ISBN: 1-4033-5113-9 (e-book)
ISBN: 1-4033-5114-7 (Paperback)

Library of Congress Control Number: 2002093109

This book is printed on acid free paper.

Printed in the United States of America
Bloomington, IN

1stBooks - rev. 08/26/02

CHAPTER ONE

A shrill ring pierced the night, waking Doc Jamison from a deep and peaceful sleep. Rubbing his eyes, he squinted at the clock on the nightstand. "One o'clock," he grumbled as he grabbed the phone.

"Doc here, can I help you?"

"Doc?"

"Yeah, who's there?"

Silence.

"C'mon, speak up. Who's calling?"

"J-J-Joe's dead, can ya come over, Doc?"

Doc's voice softened. "Sandra, that you?"

"Yeah." Her voice sounded faint and broken.

"My God, Sandra! Joe's dead? How'd he die?"

She didn't reply.

The line went dead.

Doc grabbed his black bag from the table and bent over to kiss his wife. She barely stirred. He caressed her long black hair. After brushing it back from her peaceful face, he kissed her forehead. Married to him all

David Huffman

these years, and accustomed to night calls, she had learned to ignore these intrusions.

He could tell that she seemed worried.

She opened her eyes and frowned. "What's wrong?"

"Gotta go."

Mary turned on the light and sat on the side of the bed. "Everything all right, Charles?"

"Something's happened at Sandra and Joe's. Be back by breakfast."

"What's happened, Charles?"

"Joe's dead."

"Oh my God, how'd he die?"

"I don't know."

"Why don't you call the sheriff, and let him take care of things?"

Charles thought for a moment. "Maybe I should, but Sandra called me, not the sheriff. She needs my help. That alcoholic, wife beating, bastard's apparently dead. I hope she didn't kill him. At least, he can't hurt her anymore."

"Charles, can I help?"

Charles put his hand on Mary's shoulder. "Go to sleep, dear. I'll tell you what happened in the morning."

Charles finished dressing and made his way down the back steps. He pulled on his galoshes and headed out toward his Jeep at the end of the driveway. The wind whipped rain in his face.

Fumbling for his keys, Charles opened the door and inserted the ignition key. The Jeep groaned, but like the old doc, it too started. He double-pumped the clutch. The gears whined, then engaged, and he drove the car down the driveway and out onto the county road toward the Baldwin's house.

Charles reached the edge of town, and a few minutes later found the driveway that leading the Baldwin home. The Baldwin collie ran along the fence, barking.

He could see Sandra through the kitchen window. Although in her early twenties, she seemed much older as she sat staring at the bedroom door.

He knocked.

"Come in," she said in a feeble voice.

Charles opened the door and entered into the kitchen. He looked her over. A large bruise and a cut covered her left eye. A trail of blood streaked down her nose and ended at the corner of her mouth.

Charles put his bag on the table. He took out a bandage and used it to wipe the blood from her face. She lifted her right arm to stop him.

"Sandra, I'm here to help you."

Her face blanched, the color of white, as she lowered her arm.

Charles examined her bruises, taking notice of her arm. He had fixed a fracture of her right arm before, but now the crooked arm indicated a new fracture.

"Where's Joe?"

"He's in the bedroom." She anxiously nodded toward the door at the end of the hall.

"Where are your kids?"

"At Sis's."

Charles placed his hand on Sandra's shoulder to steady his nerves, as well as hers. He walked slowly toward the bedroom. As he approached, he smelled the stench of alcohol mixed with vomit. He opened the door.

"My God!"

Joe lay face up on the bed. He had a hole in the right side of his face, below his eye.

Blood and brains painted the wall above the bed's headboard.

Charles forced himself to enter the bedroom. He looked over the room. Joe's body stretched sideways on the bed. A pistol lay on the floor. Charles stood, for what seemed like an eternity, trying to think, to remember the past, and to decide what to do.

Clearly, there were two victims here, both Joe and Sandra. At least, Joe had beaten Sandra for the last time. Charles thought, she wouldn't suffer anymore at Joe's hands, but, if she killed him, does she have to suffer the consequences of tonight? After all, if he and others in the town had done something to stop Joe, this might not have happened.

He paused. Sandra certainly had every right to want Joe dead, but Charles didn't even know if Sandra knew how to use a gun. If she did, he had to do something to protect her. How could he help her? Moreover, what about his dilemma if he covered things up? As the town doctor, Charles had never lied or misrepresented anything, but he knew Sandra shouldn't suffer anymore. He thought, my God, what could I do?

He surveyed the room again. If he changed things, how would he do it and make it look like it had happened that way? He wanted to make sure that the sheriff wouldn't notice any changes.

Joe lay askew on the bed. Joe's pistol lay at the foot of the bed. Blood seemed everywhere. Whatever he did, he had to be careful not to get Joe's blood on his hands.

Charles took his coat off and draped it on a chair beside the bed. He took his stethoscope from his black bag and slung it around his neck. He then took rubber gloves and slowly put them on, watching Joe's body for any sign of movement. He felt for Joe's carotid, no pulse. He took the earpieces from his shoulder, and adjusted the end of the stethoscope to fit his ears. Then, he put the diaphragm of the scope on Joe's chest. No heartbeat. He looked at his watch. Three-thirty in the morning. He made a mental note of the time of death.

His doctor's chores finished, he moved into his role to help Sandra. Picking up Joe's legs, he moved them toward the middle of the bed. Satisfied with their position, he grabbed Joe under the arms and lifted the body toward the head of the bed so Joe's position would correspond with the blood stains smeared on the wall.

Satisfied with the position of Joe's body, he took a handkerchief from the breast pocket of his coat. Even though he had on rubber gloves, he wrapped the handkerchief around the gun. Carefully, he raised Joe's right arm, and put the pistol in Joe's hand. Charles then closed Joe's fingers around the handle, and placed the hand with the gun beside Joe's head.

Breathing heavily, Charles went to the bathroom sink and ripped off his gloves. He stuffed them into his pocket, then scrubbed his hands. Looking at Joe's body, he backed slowly out of the room.

He found Sandra, wide-eyed, where he had left her in the kitchen. In a soft voice belying his apprehension, he said, "I need to call the sheriff."

Sandra nodded.

"Sheriff, Doc Jamison here. Joe shot himself. Yeah, I'm here with Sandra. Yeah Sheriff, she's all right. Better come right over."

They sat quietly, and waited. Tears ran down Sandra's blanched face. Charles broke the silence. "You're in pain." He reached into his black bag, shook pills from a bottle, and handed them to her with a glass of water. "This'll take the edge off."

She shook her head.

"Please, Sandra, take these. They'll help you relax."

"No, I want to stay alert."

They let the sheriff in through the kitchen door. Jacob Leiker, a heavyset man and about fifty years old, had been the elected sheriff of Smith County five years earlier, in 1962. A tall lanky man, he took pride in his dress. Despite the night, his shirt and pants had no wrinkles. Charles could almost see himself in the shine of the sheriff's black alligator cowboy boots. The sheriff's wide-brimmed hat covered his balding head. Bushy thick eyebrows came together at the midline and accentuated the gap between his two front teeth when he talked. His square jaw gave way to a stubby neck with an open collar that exposed a clean pressed T-shirt. A carved Leather belt with shiny bullets—there were none missing—held a 44-caliber pistol in a leather holster at his side. If it weren't for his belly that lapped over his belt, he would be perfect.

Despite his impeccable appearance, Charles knew the sheriff wasn't up to date with law enforcement techniques. During the past five years, there had been only one suspicious death in Smithville. However, he did know the sheriff's did his best, and Charles counted on that.

All business, the sheriff tipped his Stetson to Sandra, and shook Charles's hand. The sheriff stomped his feet and took off his galoshes. Throwing his coat on the chair, he blew into his hands. "My God, it's wet out there. Where's Joe?"

Charles pointed toward the bedroom door. He followed the sheriff, down the hall. Joe's eyes, bulging and grotesque, still stared blankly at the ceiling.

The sheriff took a pen from his shirt pocket and pushed it deftly into the pistol barrel. Joe's hand, stiff from early rigor mortis, clung tightly to the gun, as though alive. The sheriff groaned as he pried Joe's stiffened fingers from the handle. He raised the gun and examined it carefully. "A police 38," he muttered. "Didn't know Joe had one of these."

Sheriff Leiker stepped back and carefully surveyed the room. He walked to the foot of the bed. He reached down, picked up a handkerchief, and held it to the light. "Whose snot rag is this?"

Charles didn't respond.

The sheriff held the handkerchief up to the light and twirled it around. He brought the cloth close to his face and sucked air through his flared nostrils.

He frowned. "Damn cold, can't smell a thing."

Charles began to sweat.

The sheriff, after looking around the room, dropped the handkerchief on the night table.

Out of the corner of his eyes, he looked at Charles. "Looks to me like Joe shot his head off, whatya think, Doc? Must've got drunk and depressed. Can't see how it happened any other way. You're the coroner, Doc, what you think?"

"Yeah." Charles felt a surge of relief. "Yeah, that's the way I see it."

The ambulance crew loaded Joe's body on a gurney and pushed the cart into their truck.

Pulling on his coat, the sheriff turned around and said to Charles, "You help Sandra, and I'll get your statements in the morning."

Charles and Sandra watched out the window as the sheriff and ambulance drove down the road and out onto the highway. Charles turned to her. "C'mon Sandra, let me get your raincoat. I'll take you over to my office and sew up those cuts and set your fracture."

He put his arm around her. "Everything will be okay. Let me help you with your coat."

She squinted into the light and cowered.

"I'm not going to hurt you. No one will hurt you anymore. Here, put this over your shoulders, it's wet outside."

Her lips cracked slightly, showing a tooth hanging from its roots.

David Huffman

"He won't hurt me again, will he?" She pleaded.

She sobbed, falling back into the chair.

"No, he won't, I'll see to that."

The phone rang and Charles picked it up. "Sandra, it's your sister. She wants to talk with you."

Her voice steadied, "Yeah, Sis, everything's okay."

Sandra hesitated, and looked up. "Sis, you wanna talk with Doc."

Charles asked, "The kids okay? I have to take your sister to the office to sew up her cuts and fix her arm. Can you come over there and pick her up?"

Sandra's eyes were wide and unblinking, as she watched him return the phone to its hook.

They trudged through the mud. He helped Sandra into the front seat, then hesitated. "Forgot my bag. Be right back. I'll make sure the lights are off and the house is locked."

Sandra nodded. "Thanks, Doc, you've been real kind."

After getting his handkerchief, Charles looked around the bedroom to make sure he hadn't forgotten anything else. Turning off the lights, he locked the door and walked back to his car.

He paused on the front porch to collect his thoughts. Lightning streaked across the southern sky. He counted slowly to six before he heard thunder. The storm clouds were almost seven miles toward the south and east. There were no clouds in the west to cover the setting nearly full moon. Moon shadows cast eerily to the east, making it hard for him to see the front of the house. For a moment, he thought he saw something move.

Charles could hear the Baldwin's dog barking in the distance. Charles could hear the horses whinnying and a cow mooing. He wondered if Sandra could take care of this place by herself. If she couldn't, Charles knew that Sandra's dad, Richard, would have to help, if she decided to keep this place.

Charles looked at his Jeep. He had purchased a maroon, wood paneled, Willys-Overland Jeep, during the first week he'd opened his practice, in the summer of 1963. The Jeep had a fold-down rear hatch for easy loading. The front bench seat of the Willys felt more comfortable than the bucket seats of the old army Jeep, which he drove in the fifties, in medical school. Since they had quit making the Willys in 1965, he had become convinced the station wagon would become an antique.

The rain, now gone, had left the road to town muddy. Charles took off his bulky gloves, and turned each hub to engage the 4-wheel drive. Every time he did this, he worried about his hands, so important to his profession. Starting the car, he pumped the clutch. Dropping the gears into low he drove slowly down the muddy road and out onto the highway, toward his office.

How many times had he gone to help Sandra? Most of the time he took care of the kids' colds. However, Sandra had had too many falls, scrapes, bruises, and fractures. Young and pretty, she always had an excuse, and he played along. After all, they lived in a small town and Joe ran the local pharmacy; Charles didn't know how he could practice without a pharmacist, so he looked the other way. Now he wished he hadn't. Perhaps, he could have prevented this.

One time he had tried to talk with Joe over coffee. Joe, always very nice when sober, had denied hurting Sandra. Charles decided not to pursue things.

Charles thought about his own life as the only doctor in Smithville. People relied on him for help. He knew they appreciated his caring and sensitive manner. Many times, however, he could provide only comfort.

A large man who prided himself in dress, he always wore a suit coat and a bow tie. He looked in the rear-view mirror. He found himself disheveled and out of character. Despite the rain and the cold, he had left his overcoat on the bedroom chair.

CHAPTER TWO

"I gotta go back to your house."

"Why?"

"It won't take long. Gotta get something."

Charles turned the Jeep around and headed back up the driveway. He went back into the house, and picked up his coat. He surveyed the bedroom. The stench of Joe's body remained.

He looked around, retrieved his coat, and sloshed through the mud back to his Jeep. Charles turned east onto Main Street. He didn't want to hurt Sandra further, so he drove slowly over the brick pavement. Since the rain had stopped, he switched off his wipers, then slowed to a gradual stop at the corner of First and Main.

Sandra stirred.

"You okay?"

"My arm hurts."

He wished she had taken the Demerol pills, or better yet, he had given her a morphine shot before they left her house. "We'll be at my office in a moment. Gotta clean the window pane, so I can see."

Lightning sliced across the southern sky. Muffled thunder followed. He glanced in the rear-view mirror, then right and left. Usually, the kids dragged up and down Main on Friday night, but the street vacant due to the late hour. Charles had worried when his son drove this street. Charles could never sleep until Jason came home safely.

He rolled down his window and with his gloved hand reached out to clean the caked mud from the front window. He groaned. "Window's too dirty to clean from inside." Reaching in the back seat, he grabbed a rag, and got out of the Jeep to clean the window.

Only six blocks long, Main Street was paved with memories. Along the street, at every half-block, dim globes on poles provided the only light. The City Council had tried several times to increase the lighting, but the town always voted down their plans. Charles felt more illumination would provide more safety, but the town preferred the old-style lamps. Change came slowly for Smithville. Would tonight modify that?

Back behind the wheel, he pumped the clutch and coaxed his Jeep into first gear. "Storm's over."

"You think so?"

"Depends on which storm," he replied, wondering if she caught the reference.

Joe's pharmacy stood in the first block on the south side of Main Street. As they drove by, they glanced at the dark building, then quickly turned their eyes away, and stared ahead.

Charles thought about Joe and his pharmacy. He thought about the soda fountain where Charles and the other men from the town often gathered for coffee each morning.

When Joe had been sober, most everyone in town liked him. When he had been drunk, he had been a mean-spirited, sewer-mouthed man, who constantly made jokes about women. Charles had worried for years about his abuse of Sandra and their kids. Now, he regretted not stepping forward and stopping Joe's abuse.

Charles's emotional control astounded him. He had changed the death scene. He didn't have any idea how Joe had died. Did Sandra do it? Had someone else shot Joe? He didn't know.

He drove past Reed's Furniture Store with its mortuary in the back. There were lights on in the back. He imagined the sheriff's deputies were off loading Joe's body into the mortuary. As he drove down Main, he passed Jacob's IGA grocery store and the Town Hall on the right side of the street.

Smithville, an old cattle town, had burned in the twenties after a fire in a saloon. The town's people, with the help of the WPA, had rebuilt the town during the depression, using limestone bricks from a quarry. He loved the strength of these buildings; they represented a constant in his changing world.

He could make out a light in the sheriff's office in the back of the Town Hall. Charles wanted to stop and see the sheriff, but Sandra needed attention, so he drove on.

They continued on to the end of Main Street and parked in front of his office. The small wooden structure had been another family's home before Charles bought and fixed up the main floor for use as his office. Although rarely occupied, the rooms upstairs were available for people who didn't want to go to the hospital, thirty miles east of Smithville.

Despite summer time, he felt a chill as he entered his office. "I'll turn up the heat," he said. Red-flocked wallpaper with floral prints covered the waiting room. Two wing-backed chairs and a worn couch bedecked the perimeter of a tattered Persian rug spread over the pine-wooden floor. At the end of the room, an inviting staircase curled up toward the second floor.

Sandra started to sit down on the couch, carefully cradling her broken right arm.

Charles gently took her by her left shoulder. "Come, let's go back to the treatment room."

He helped her up on the examination table. "Can you sit here a minute?" He went back into his office and opened a closet, then took out a clean shirt. He slipped off his shirt, and threw it in a clothes hamper. He washed and dried his hands, combed his hair, and after putting on the clean shirt, he tied his bow tie.

He found Sandra lying on the table. After examining the cut over her eyebrow, he opened her eyelids and flashed his penlight in her eyes. Her pupils reacted normally. He sighed in relief. Despite the blow to her head, she had no signs of a concussion. He wiped the blood from her nose and mouth.

Sandra pulled away, and covered her mouth.

"I can't fix your tooth, but Harry will be in his office before long. I'll have him pull the tooth and check your mouth."

Carefully he palpated her neck, and listened to her heart and lungs. He felt her abdomen. "That hurt?"

She shook her head.

Then he examined her arm. "Bad break. At least, your skin's intact over the break. I'll give you a shot to deaden the pain before I set the fracture."

He grabbed a bottle of phenobarbital and morphine. He took a syringe from a tray beside the table and fitted it with a metal needle from a tray of soapy water on the desk. Drawing the medicine, he tapped the glass syringe and pushed air bubbles out the top. He then plunged the needle deftly into her arm, and pushed in the medicine.

Sandra grimaced.

"Sorry. It'll make it easier to set the fracture."

"I know. It hurts though."

Her eyelids closed, and her head sagged. He gently touched her shoulder. "Sandra?" She didn't respond. He grabbed her shoulder with his left hand. He held her wrist firmly above her thumb, and pulled until he could hear the bones scrape together. Satisfied that the bones were in their best alignment, he wrapped her arm with plaster of Paris.

After sewing up her facial cuts, he sat back and watched her. He thought about the night and his dilemma created by changing the death scene. He knew that he had done the right thing.

Sandra stirred, opened her eyes, and combed her fingers through her hair with her good hand. She took a deep breath and lifted her head. "Guess I fell asleep," she said. Her head jerked to the side with an involuntary tic.

"You okay?"

"I-I think so."

"How's your head and arm?"

She strained to move her arm, but she couldn't lift her arm because of the heavy cast. "Hurts a lot." She grimaced.

Charles took her arm carefully and examined her fingers for blood supply. "The arm's okay. I'll call your sister, and tell her she can pick you up. I need to get home, and clean up before patients arrive in the morning."

She reached up with her left hand and started to touch his shoulder, then drew back. Charles smiled. The appreciation he now saw in her eyes compensated him more than money, and gave him satisfaction that he had helped her.

Sandra said, "What's going to happen to me?"

Charles patted her head. "Calm down. Everything will be all right."

He knew he was lying. Today, she would have to tell her children that their father was dead. No telling how they would react. She had a funeral to arrange. Maybe worse than anything, she would have to deal with the suspicion and judgment of the community. Along with their pity, they would have endless questions. Moreover, what about his own questions? If Sandra did kill Joe, could she keep it from the town? Could she keep it from her children? If she blurted everything out and confessed, would he be honor-bound to confess his own guilt? Would he lose the respect of the people he had served these many years? More importantly, would he have to spend time in jail?

He struggled to recall what he and the sheriff had said in front of her. "Sandra, what do you remember about last night?"

She struggled to remember. "I had just put the kids to bed when Joe came home. Like usual, he had been drinking. He always drank after leaving the store. He scowled at me, then he yelled that he wasn't going to eat that slop. He threw the dinner on the floor and screamed. He called me a bitch and told me to clean it up."

Outraged, Charles muttered under his breath. "That S-O-B."

"I put my arm up, but he grabbed and twisted it." Red-faced, she cried. "I heard my arm break."

"What happened next?"

"I must've passed out. When I woke up, I couldn't hear anything. I looked for Joe. I saw vomit in the hall outside of the bedroom. I found him on the bed. I called you after that."

"Where were the kids?"

"I don't know."

"You told me they were at your sis's."

Sandra frowned. "Did I? Yeah, I guess they were. I must've called her before I called you." She twirled her hair with her left hand. "That's right, I called her. She told me the kids had run to her house."

"Did you hear a gunshot?"

"I must've."

Charles had doubts about her story. He decided to take a break, and got up and walked over to the window. "It's stuffy in here. Need some air?" He cracked the window and took a deep breath. "You want something to drink? I have a soda in the fridge."

She nodded as he took out a cola and popped off the cap with the bottle opener, then handed it to her. She took a long sip, coughed a bit, and finished her drink.

"Thanks, I am real thirsty, and bone-tired." She closed her eyes and drifted off again.

Charles looked her over. They'd have to finish their conversation later. Her memory seemed incomplete.

He thought back four and a half years ago to the first time he had met her at Jacob's IGA Grocery Store. Charles had only been in town for six months when they met. Sandra had been eighteen at the time.

He learned that she had always been brimful of life and a real happy child. She'd grown up on a farm south of town, and never lived anywhere but with her family and Joe.

At fifteen, still in high school, she had met Joe at a barn dance. They started going steady right away. Joe finished high school and went to the university to study pharmacy. He had been wild in high school, drinking a lot of beer, always in a fight.

Everyone hoped Joe would settle down; indeed, when he came home from the university, he seemed gentler. He was good to Sandra. She got pregnant, so they married. Joe appeared really proud of his new wife and family. They always came to church dressed in their Sunday best. Charles and the rest of the town relaxed their worry. They seemed like a model family.

Charles knew Sandra's dad, Richard Thompson, didn't trust Joe.

Charles thought back to a recent encounter with Richard.

******

Last month at the Co-op, Richard had pushed open the door and stomped his feet on the rug. "Glad to have the moisture, it'll help the wheat grow."

Richard took off his slicker and hat and hung them on a wall hook. He ran his fingers through his graying crew cut. Despite being nearly fifty, he had large biceps under the sleeves of his work shirt. The corded muscles in his forearms flexed under a tattoo of an Eagle, Globe, and Anchor. His flannel shirt opened above his overalls, exposing his sunburned neck.

His hands were leathered, scarred, and tough. A Marine before coming back to the farm, he avoided confrontation, but everyone

David Huffman

in town knew he had killed a few Japs on Iwo Jima.

"Need some chicken feed and kerosene," he said in his gravelly voice. "How you doing, Doc?" He looked Charles squarely in the eye, then reached for the money. "Almost forgot, need a box of twelve-gauge shells and bullets for my handgun."

Ralph, the manager of the Co-op looked up. "What kinda shot, Richard?"

"Double O buck," he said, "Magnum load for my twelve gauge. And standard shells for my 38."

The store manager looked worried. "What the hell ya gonna shoot?"

Richard grinned. "Might use them to kill my hogs this fall. Or jus use um for target practice. Jus might pop one of those varmints that keep buggin' me."

Richard gathered his supplies and started out the door. He turned slowly to Charles. He lowered his voice to a confidential tone. "I'm really gettin' worried about Sandy. Doc, you know. You've fixed her broken arms several times in the past. I can't figure out why she's been hurt so often. I'm not getting the straight skinny from her. I wish I hadn't let her marry that son-of-a-bitch. If that bastard hurts my baby again, it'll be the last time. You can count on that."

He rattled the box of shotgun shells menacingly, and stomped out the door.

Charles started after him, but stopped and turned slowly to Ralph. "Don't think Richard has much love for Joe. I'm worried about Sandra and the kids. In fact, I'm worried about all of them."

Ralph nodded. "I guess a dad's gotta do what a dad's gotta do. Galls him bad him being a Marine and having to watch someone beat up on his own daughter."

******

A loud banging at the door brought Charles back to the present. "Must be your sis. I'll let her in, and help you out to her car."

Charles opened the door and stared at Barbara, Sandra's sister. "She's in the exam room, still a bit groggy from the pain medicines." He looked her over, wondering what Barbara might know about the night.

"Sandra's okay, isn't she?"

"Yes, I set her fracture and sewed up her cuts."

"What happened?"

"You don't know?"

"Sandra called. Said Joe's dead. How'd it happen?"

Charles persisted, "When did she call?"

"Doc, I'm cold. Can I come in?"

"Of course, sorry."

They found Sandra sitting on the side of the table. When she saw her sister, she struggled to stand up, staggering for a moment. After Charles helped catch her, she gained her balance, then hugged Barbara as they both wept.

Barbara brushed a tear from Sandra's eye. "You okay, Sis?"

"I'm okay, I think. Aren't I, Doc?"

"You'll be fine."

Barbara pushed Sandra away from her and looked her over. "He ain't gonna hurt you anymore, Sis. No more."

"The kids. They okay?"

"They're fine. John's watching them, but he's gotta go to work. We need to get home."

She turned to Charles. "You need us any more?"

"No, I'll talk with the sheriff. If we need to talk to Sandra more, we'll do it in the morning."

Charles walked the two women to their car. He watched them drive down Main. They turned right on Sixth Street. That's curious, he thought, Barbara lives on the south side of town, but they headed north towards Sandra's house. They probably needed some clothes for her and her kids.

Charles turned the lights off and locked the office. He drove west on Main and turned right on Fourth. After a couple of blocks, he turned the Jeep east and headed toward Sandra's house.

Sure enough, they were there. He stopped and looked at the house, but he couldn't make out any movement. He thought about going inside to see if he could help, but changed his mind and headed home.

At five-thirty in the morning, Charles sensed the quiet, eerie side of Smithville. He generally enjoyed this time of day when few people were up and about. But things were different now. He felt uncomfortable. Until tonight, he had always told the truth. After all, as a doctor, he had to be honest. However, tonight, in that moment when he saw Joe's body, he had reacted and changed things.

　　He thought Sandra shot Joe. Maybe Richard shot Joe. Were there others who had a motive?

　　Steam rose from the center of the road, obscuring his vision as he drove down Main toward his house. He found his familiar street, and turned on the tree-lined driveway. The trees were fifteen-feet tall, and usually provided protection from the storm.

CHAPTER THREE

Sandra and Barbara watched Doc's Jeep pass their house slowly and turn at the corner.

"Guess he's headed home."

Quietly, they edged back toward the bedroom and opened the door. The bedroom had ghastly feel with Joe gone. Nevertheless, his blood remained. The sheets lay askew. Blood and brains stained the wall.

Sandra gasped. "I thought you said someone would clean up." She sat down, and looked at the bed. Her face red, she blurted, "I want to burn this bed. Although it's where my girls were conceived, that's where he beat me." She pointed at the bed, then turned away, tears filling her eyes. "That's where he died."

"Sandra, not now. Let's get out of here."

Sandra screamed, "I don't know why nobody did anything to stop him. I couldn't leave cause I couldn't feed the girls without him. He'd kill me if I left him."

"I know how you feel."

"No, you don't! You don't know how I feel. You'll never know how I feel. You know what I think? I think this town looked the other way, and put up with him just because he ran the pharmacy. I don't think anyone cared about me or my kids, not even you and Dad."

"Sis, we love you. You know that. We didn't know what to do."

Sandra looked wide-eyed at her sister. "Well, it's over." She grabbed a handkerchief from the dresser and blew her nose. "You, Doc, and the sheriff think Joe killed himself."

"Maybe he did. Poor dear, you must be in shock. I bet you can't even remember my coming over to get the kids."

Sandra stared at Barbara, confused. "I don't remember much." Sandra sobbed, slowly at first. Soon her body began to shake.

Barbara put her arm around Sandra. "Joe was a mean man, and what's done is done. You keep quiet about things. I'll take care of you."

"I know, Sis."

Sandra got a bag from the closet and packed some clothes. "Can you get something for the girls? I don't ever want to come back here again."

Barbara nodded. "I'd feel the same."

They packed three bags. The furnace fan and the refrigerator kept turning on and off, interrupting the eerie quiet. Sandra grabbed a towel, and held it under the sink. She slowly wrung out the water, and wiped the headboard clean.

"Don't. Someone will clean it up."

Sandra dropped the towel. Shivering, she cried softly.

Barbara patted her back. "It's okay. Everything will be okay." She surveyed the room. Satisfied they had everything, she led Sandra back into the kitchen. "Sit here for a while; I need to check one more thing."

Barbara returned to the bedroom. In the corner, near his closet, Joe had a desk with a typewriter on it. She opened the drawer and took out a piece of his stationery.

She typed a note:

I can't go on anymore. Life is sad and no one cares.

My busines is failing. I am a failure. I'm sorry.

Don't think badly of me. I tried. Joe Baldwin

Barbara left the note in the typewriter. She hoped the sheriff hadn't seen the typewriter earlier.

Barbara helped Sandra with her coat. They walked down the walkway to her Scout. Barbara said, "Everything will be all right."

The sun peeked above the trees. Barbara had the defroster on full blast. She wiped the inside of the fogged up window with her sleeve.

They drove slowly down Main past the pharmacy. Sandra stared at the building. "What'll become of the business?"

How will we survive?"

"Don't worry about that now, Sandy. We can take care of that later. First, we gotta get you to my house. After that, we gotta make arrangements to bury Joe. Have you called Dad?"

"No, I'll call him from your house."

Barbara helped Sandra out of her Scout and into her house. She then went back to get the bags. As she walked back into the house, she heard Sandra talking on the phone.

"Dad." Sandra sobbed into the phone, "Joe's dead, killed with a gun. The sheriff thinks he killed himself. At least, that's what Doc Jamison told me."

David Huffman

CHAPTER FOUR

Exhausted and hoping for quiet, Charles drove up his circular driveway. As he got closer to his house, he could make out a strange vehicle, blocking his access.

"Oh no! Not another problem!" He complained as he turned off his headlights.

Nothing moved.

Charles fumbled for a penlight in his black bag, then pointed the dim light at the vehicle. A VW minibus. He couldn't see anyone in or around it. With the penlight pointed straight ahead, he opened his door cautiously and went to investigate.

Yellow, red, and chipped badly, the VW had a large peace symbol painted in black covering the back window. Charles pointed the light inside the bus. A torn sleeping bag lay on top of a sheet-less mattress. For a moment, he thought he could see someone, but the bag didn't move. Above the mattress hung an old New York baseball hat. That's familiar, he thought.

The thought of someone driving this eyesore nauseated him. What would his neighbors think? More than anything, the VW, and all it represented, offended him. Charles knew times were changing. Kids were rebelling. Nonetheless, he couldn't accept, let alone understand, the younger generation.

Charles brushed his sleeves and straightened his back. He regained his composure. Back into his doctor's role, he reasoned, perhaps someone is injured, pregnant, or has a child with a fever, and has stopped to get his help.

As he walked around the front of the van, he caught the whiff of a sweet smell. He squinted, and then rubbed his eyes. He could make out the glow from the end of a cigarette and the outline of a man on the front porch.

He stopped in his tracks.

"Who's there?"

The man stood, and blew out a puff of smoke.

"Dad?"

"Jason? Is that you?"

Jason flicked his cigarette into the driveway. Charles quickly crushed out the lighted butt with his shoe.

Charles sucked in his breath. His heart pounded wildly. He hadn't seen his son in two years.

Charles pointed his penlight in Jason's direction. Jason's straight, dirty hair fell around his shoulders. Although they were the same height, Jason's shoulders slouched, creating the impression of a smaller man. A pack of cigarettes folded in the rolled sleeve of his tie-dyed T-shirt, emphasized his muscular arms. His bell-bottom, worn at the knees, barely covered his scuffed Converse basketball shoes.

Charles wanted to grab and hug his son. After all, he hadn't seen him for two years. Something held him back. He looked Jason over.

What has happened to my son? When he left, he had been clean and had a flat top. Now this. What have I done to deserve this?

Jason broke the silence. "Aren't you glad to see me?"

"Jason, is that you? I didn't expect you. You left so angry. I-I don't know what to say."

"You were never at a loss for words. Why don't you just say you're glad to see me?"

Trying to think, Charles stammered. "I- We're happy you're alive."

"God damn it, I wish I hadn't come home. You're not happy to see me, are you?"

"Don't swear at me. I'm shocked to see you. You've changed. You've caught me off guard." Charles sat down on the porch steps. He clasped his hands to keep from shaking as he stared at Jason.

"I guess I should have written, or at least called. You pissed me off, so I left. I figured we'd never talk again, so why make the effort."

Charles straightened his bow tie. "I remember. You slammed the door when you walked out and never looked back."

Charles and Jason sat on a bench in the front yard. Charles looked at the pack of cigarettes rolled in Jason's sleeve. He started to make a comment, then thought better, and kept quiet.

They sat side by side in silence, each sensing the other's tension.

A gush of wind rustled the leaves, breaking the silence. Jason brushed his hair back. As quickly as the wind came, it died down. The growing, undulating, clamor of the nightly locust chorus replaced the wind.

They listened.

Charles mused. "Curious isn't it? Those locusts live underground for seventeen years, then surface, mate, and die within a few days.

Jason said, "Strange all right." He paused for a moment, then continued. "Hope I can stay longer than a few days."

Charles gazed at Jason. "You by yourself?"

"Yeah, just me. Can I stay a spell?"

Charles looked his son over. Jason scared him. He knew very little about his son. Where had his son been since he left home? He wanted to accept him with open arms, but Jason confused him. Why is he here now? Why tonight?

Charles cleared his throat. "Sure, you can stay. Your mother refused to change your room, hoping you'd come back."

Jason grabbed a duffle bag out of the back of the VW, and they walked up to the house and onto the front porch. They opened the door to find Mary standing in her nightgown at the bottom of the stairs.

Rubbing sleep from her eyes, she said, "Jason, is that you?"

"Yes, Mom."

"Oh my God, you've come home." She looked at Charles, then at Jason. "Our baby's come home." She ran toward Jason.

Jason dropped his bag and wrapped his arms around his mother. They kissed and held each other tight.

Mary looked at Charles with tearing, red eyes. "Charles, Jason's home."

They hugged.

Mary held Jason at arm's length. "Let me look at you. Why didn't you call?"

Jason replied, "Didn't know what to say. Just decided to come home."

Charles said, "Well, we're glad your home.

Mary interrupted, "Charles! No inquisition. We'll talk in the morning. Tonight, I want to savor the joy of his coming home."

Jason yawned. "I'm tired, Mom."

"Aren't we all? You know where your room is. Get some sleep. We'll talk in the morning."

Charles watched Jason climb the stairs.

Mary said, "Isn't it great, our son is home?"

"Yes. It's great."

"Charles, what happened at Joe's?"

"Joe killed himself."

"You're kidding. Joe?"

"I'm afraid so. With his 38."

"He's too arrogant and too much a coward to have ended things that way, Charles."

Charles looked shocked. "I don't understand."

"You won't see me shedding any tears at his funeral. I say good riddance, but I doubt he killed himself."

Stunned, Charles stared at her. "What do you mean good riddance?"

"Joe was a mean drunk who beat his wife and children. Everyone knows; don't tell me you didn't know."

"Yeah, I knew, but I didn't expect it to end this way. Our town doesn't need violence. We don't need some investigation to come here and pry."

"I don't know what you mean, come here and pry."

"Every time something happens, those guys in the county seat come here and get into our business. We don't have anything to hide. I don't like someone looking over our shoulders. Never know what they might find out."

"What are you afraid of?"

"Never mind, forget I said anything."

Mary looked him over. "Charles, tell me what happened."

Charles recounted the story about going to the house and finding Sandra with a broken arm and cuts on her face. He told how he found Joe dead in the bedroom. There would be a coroner's inquest on Monday, and he would serve as the county coroner. Charles didn't tell his wife what he had done. He wanted to tell her, but not tonight.

Charles gave her a squeeze, and then pointed up the stairs. "You go on to bed, dear. I need to unwind. Think I'll read a bit in the library."

His favorite room, this oak-paneled library held wall-to-wall books. A Persian rug and an old oak library table gave the room a cozy feel. Beside the desk, a mahogany table supported a large <u>Webster's Dictionary</u>.

Although he rarely needed to look up a word, he liked the ambiance the dictionary added to the room.

Charles thumbed through the dictionary until his finger came to rest on the word "honest." Was he free from fraud, or deception?

An avid reader, Charles loved mystery novels the most, especially stories by Agatha Christie. At times, he fancied himself as a modern Poirot. Now he had a real need to become that Poirot he admired. He needed to find out who killed Joe.

He loved this library. He could escape the outside world in this sanctuary. Would tonight change that? He examined the wall of books. He ran his finger along the middle row, searching for a book on ethics, hoping to find direction and advice.

CHAPTER FIVE

Sunlight streamed through the library window, waking Charles from a restless sleep. He rubbed his eyes and stretched his arms. Although he often fell asleep reading, he never felt rested after sleeping in this chair. He looked at his watch. Seven-thirty. He had only a half hour until patients would arrive at his office.

He climbed the stairs, showered, and dressed.

Mary stirred. He kissed her.

"You leaving?"

"Yeah. Office opens at eight. Should be home by noon."

"Call if you're going to be late."

Charles looked out the window at the VW. Uncertain how he would communicate with his son, he was nonetheless happy to have Jason home.

On his way to the office, Charles stopped by the Co-op, struggling to remember the type of shells Richard bought that day last week. Last night, he thought Sandra had killed Joe.

Now Richard, and possibly her sister could have done it. He bit his lip.

Charles saw Ralph pull the blinds and flip the sign to open the Co-op. Charles banged on the front door. "Open up."

"Keep your pants on, Doc, I'll be right there."

Hoping nobody would see him, Charles looked nervously up and down the street. Calm down, he thought, you've nothing to be afraid of. After all, the sheriff agreed that Joe had killed himself. Charles rationalized that his actions were for the good of the town. Clearly, in his opinion, he had acted for Sandra's benefit.

Ralph turned the lock. "You're here mighty early, Doc. Anything wrong?"

"Joe's dead."

"Jesus that really surprises me. How'd it happen?"

"I'm not sure. The sheriff thinks Joe shot himself."

Ralph looked pensive. "I gotta admit Joe was mean. Everyone knew he beat Sandra and the kids. I can't say I'll miss him, He never paid his bills on time. But, I don't quite buy him killing himself, too much a coward."

"That's what Mary said." Charles hesitated for a moment. "Do you remember Richard in here, buying some shotgun shells? Can you recall what kind of shells he bought?"

"Twelve-gauge I think, let me look." He pulled a book out from under the counter and ran his finger down the page. "Ya remember what day?"

"A week ago Thursday, I think."

Ralph opened the ledger, thumbed back to the previous week, and ran his finger down the side of the page. "Here it is. Yeah, he bought some twelve-gauge shells for his shotgun and also a box of shells for a 38."

"A 38 pistol."

"Yeah."

"I thought he only needed shotgun shells."

"Needed those, too, but here it is, he bought shells for a police special 38."

Charles struggled to remember the gun he saw at the Baldwin's, a police special, or a regular 38. He shrugged his shoulders, for he didn't know guns that well anyway, so what made him think he could tell the difference.

David Huffman

"Thanks, I gotta get to my office."

"Hey, how 'bout coffee later?"

"Not today."

He drove slowly past Joe's pharmacy. A light shown in a back room. He couldn't remember seeing a light when he drove past earlier with Sandra. Maybe it was Beth, Joe's assistant. Must be, he thought, she always comes early to get the store ready for the day. She wouldn't know about Joe, so Charles decided to tell her.

Charles parked his Jeep and peered in the front window. No movement. Suddenly, the light went off. Charles knocked loudly. No answer. He shrugged, and started back toward the car, when he heard a car in the alley. He ran to the side of the building in time to see Richard's pickup turn the corner and head south.

Charles ran back to the Jeep to follow him. Something is fishy here. Why is Richard in the store? What is he looking for? A chill ran up Charles's spine.

Charles didn't Richard to see him, so he kept well behind Richard's truck. Richard turned south on First Street toward Barbara's house. That's strange. Maybe Barbara or Sandra had called Richard, and he had come over to be with them. Charles couldn't think of any good reason Richard would be in the pharmacy. Charles looked at his watch as he headed for his office. Eight-fifteen. He floored the accelerator, not wanting to keep his patients waiting.

He surveyed the full waiting room. Nobody looked sick, except for Bob, who sat in the corner holding his stomach. Bob and Joe best were drinking buddies. Charles decided to see Bob first.

Charles grunted a perfunctory greeting to those in the room, and headed back to the exam rooms. As he rounded the corner, Nurse Gertrude, standing with her hands on her hips, blocked his way, her wide body as rigid as her starched white uniform. "What the hell happened here last night?"

Charles sucked in a deep breath, and backed up. "Glad to see you, too, Gertrude." Topping off her robust physique, she sported a dainty nurse cap that covered her graying hair. He didn't know what he would do without her. Because, more than anything, Gertrude was a great nurse. At times, however, she really intimidated him.

"This room's a mess. The hogs have a cleaner place. I stayed late last night cleaning up, now look at the place."

Charles tried to look contrite. "Sorry, didn't have time to clean up. I fixed Sandra's fracture and sewed up her facial cuts."

"That bastard hit her, again?"

"For the last time."

"Whatever do you mean?"

"Joe's dead."

"How?"

Charles recounted the story. He hesitated, and then he told Gertrude that it looked like Joe shot himself.

A voice came from behind them. "I don't think so."

Charles whirled around to see Bob standing in the door.

Bob continued. "Can't remember for sure, but Joe and I were out drinking at the Brass Rail until at least eleven. We were both so drunk neither of us could drive, so Joe walked home. I'm not sure how I got home, but I think I drove. Must've passed out. I woke up this morning with a headache and this damn pain in my stomach."

"Bob, you never can get your story straight, particularly when you've been drinking. I doubt you were with Joe at all last night." Charles chided. "Come back here and sit on the table so I can see what's wrong with you." Charles and Gertrude exchanged knowing glances.

"I do too remember. At least, I can remember some things. Go ask Richard, Sandra's dad. He saw us at the bar."

Charles turned his head to avoid Bob's nauseating breath. "What do you mean? Richard drinking at the bar?" He doesn't drink-not that I know of."

"Well, he saw both of us. He came over and talked to Joe, something about Joe's drinking and not being a good husband. They yelled at each other. Then, Richard grabbed Joe by the shirt, lifted him up with one hand, and shook his other fist in Joe's face. My God, he scared me, what with that Semper Fi on his flexed arm. I almost peed in my pants, thinking he's goin' to hurt us both."

Charles looked at Gertrude, and then at Bob. "What time did Richard leave?"

"About ten-thirty, I think, don't know. When I'm drunk, I lose track of time, you know. God, my stomach hurts. Get me a basin; I'm goin' to throw up."

Gertrude reached over for the emesis basin, but she didn't get the basin in time. Bob let loose with a loud retching sound, and then vomited, projected food from the last twenty-four hours onto the far wall. Both Gertrude and Charles jumped back. Gertrude grabbed a towel and covered Bob's head. From behind, she put one hand on his stomach while Charles reached for a basin. In an instant, however, Bob vomited again. Unlike the first time, he vomited a massive amount bright, red blood.

Bob's eyes rolled back in his head, and he belched a stale, ghastly smell.

Despite their best efforts, Bob collapsed and died.

CHAPTER SIX

Charles slumped in the chair beside the exam table. Gertrude scurried around the room, cleaning as she went. From time to time, they both looked at Bob.

Gertrude washed Bob's body. "He looks mighty peaceful. Hard to believe his life was so tough."

Charles replied, "Yeah, I guess so."

He looked Bob's body over. Bob's hand had a black smudge between his thumb and index finger. Charles picked up the hand, and sniffed it. He couldn't smell anything but blood. Charles dropped Bob's hand, glancing at Gertrude. She looked the other way. Good.

Gertrude said, "We gotta clean up this mess before we can see anyone else. Go on, get outta here, never knew a doc who liked to clean up after someone died. Go on, I'll clean up." She threw her hands in the air. "What a mess. There's no way I can do this by myself. Gotta call my sister, maybe she'll help. You go on and do what you gotta do.

David Huffman

I'll tell the others they'll have to come back later."

Charles heard the groans from the waiting room. "What'll I do with Mike? He needs an excuse to get out of work."

Gertrude said, "Stuff it, Wanda. Keep your pants on. Doc'll write ya an excuse. Just take Mike home."

Charles picked up the phone and dialed 4356. "Sheriff, Doc here. I have another body." Charles recounted the story of Bob's death.

After he put the phone down, he realized Gertrude stood behind him, looking suspiciously. "Didn't tell him about what Bob said before he died, did ya?"

"No, Bob never told the truth. So, I didn't believe him."

"Bob wasn't covering up. I thought he tried to tell the truth. Besides, maybe he knew he was dying, and dying people always tell the truth before they go."

Charles looked down and away from her gaze.

"Charles, what's going on? Look me in the eyes. I can tell when you're covering something. Who killed Joe? Did he kill himself, or did someone else kill him?"

"I'm not sure. I need to go talk to Richard and find out what he knows. If anyone needs me, I'm going to drive out south of town to see if Richard's home."

"Why don't you call him first?"

"Good idea." Charles rang Richard's farm. "No answer. Must be out in the field. Think I'll drive out, and try to find him."

Charles hurried out the back door so fast he forgot to get his coat. After starting his Jeep, he stretched up to look at himself in the rear-view mirror. "My God, you're falling apart." He straightened his bow tie. He had no comb, so all he ran his fingers through his disheveled hair and patted down his cowlick.

Charles headed onto Main. He had to talk with Richard. Then maybe he would learn the truth about what happened to Joe.

First, however, Charles stopped by Reed's Furniture Store to tell Reed Johnson, the town undertaker, about Bob. He hoped they had enough room for another body. Charles could never get used to death.

Charles walked to the back of the store and into the mortuary, where the pungent smell of embalming solution replaced the sweet odor of oak furniture.

Joe lay covered with a white sheet, on the metal table.

Charles pulled back the sheet. Despite the grotesque wounds, Joe seemed at peace. Charles would have to do an autopsy, later, when he could get help.

Charles climbed behind the wheel, pushed the transmission into low, and headed out of town.

At the six-mile marker, Charles sat for a moment, trying to remember the way to Richard's farm. After looking both ways, he started into the intersection. Out of the corner of his eye, he saw a cloud of dust, approaching at break-neck speed. He slammed the brakes in time to miss a red pickup, screaming through the intersection. Damn, he thought, his hands trembling so hard he could barely hold the wheel. I almost bought it myself.

His memory flashed back to four years ago, when a car with three teenagers hit a truck head on, and crashed into the side of the ditch. The kids had been out joy riding after playing basketball.

One thing for sure, this intersection, with its tall grass blocking the view of cross traffic, was very dangerous.

Charles had come out with the undertaker to pronounce the kids, and to help clean up. They were Jason's friends. He thanked God that Jason had had chores at home, and he and Mary had refused to let Jason go with his friends. Charles had refused to look at the boy's body. That way, he would never have to answer all of Jason's questions about the accident.

Charles collected his thoughts, wiped his brow, and turned right toward Richard's farm. When he got to the crest of the hill, he pulled over for a moment to gather his composure. To the south and west, the fields of golden wheat stretched as far as he could see. He wished his life could be as simple as those who farmed this land. There were too many things going on. He needed to think things over.

He got out of his Jeep and walked to the right of the road, to his favorite hideaway on the top of the hill. Even though it had rained hard in town, the rain hadn't changed things much up here. Parched dry, the hillside grasses were already brown from the summer sun. As he shuffled toward the crest of the hill, dust jumped up from his feet.

A large limestone rock outcropping dominated the hilltop. Charles loved to look for fossils in the limestone. He decided to sit for a moment and to think through the events of the past twelve hours.

As he sat on the top of the rock, surveying the town, Charles recalled the last time he had come up here. That had been three months ago. Earlier that night, he had responded to one of Sandra's many calls.

He remembered Sandra, with her broken body and spirit, as she tried to explain what had happened. They both knew different. Like so many times before, she was bruised and battered. Yet somehow, he had been unable to confront Joe and stop the abuse.

That night, after he had set her fracture, Charles had driven up here to think. He needed to be alone. He almost drove back down to the Baldwin's house to confront Joe. Why hadn't he? Charles put his hands on his face and began sobbing. If only he had told someone of his suspicions, maybe things would be different.

As he sat on the rock, he remembered staying up there that night until the sunrise. Like this morning, the first rays of sun were streaming behind rain clouds in the east. He recalled watching the sun lighting up the town. The first rays of light caressed the steeples of the Methodist and Catholic churches. Then, gradually, he could make out the Town Hall, and then the rest of the town's rooftops. At that moment, convinced he could see his house, he watched the morning mist settled over everything. Then, the mist began to fade by evaporating slowly from the town. Finally, he could see his home, and he wondered about Mary.

In the solitude of this place, he usually felt peace.

However, today, he didn't feel peace. Last night, he had betrayed a sacred trust, a trust always to be truthful. If only he had left things alone.

In his cover-up, had he made it impossible to find the real killer? No one but Charles knew he had lied. Nonetheless, he knew he couldn't live with himself unless he told the truth.

What would people think of him? What would Mary think? Would she still love him? Would she trust him?

Down on the road, a man waved his hands frantically and yelled, "Doc, Gertrude said you'd be out this way. My woman's in labor and the midwife is having trouble delivering my baby. Come quick, we need your help."

Charles hurried down the hill.

"Where are they?" Breathing heavily, Charles held his side. "Say again, what's wrong?"

"It's my wife, Doc. She's delivering, and the baby won't come out."

"I'll follow you."

They sped east a mile then South to a small road that led back up to a farmhouse. The midwife stood on the porch. "Hurry, Doc. I thought I could handle it, but she's breech."

Charles turned to the farmer. "Wait here. I'll see what I can do."

After a while, Charles sauntered out of the house, and put his arm around the farmer. "Congratulations, you have a new son."

The farmer broke down and cried. "How's my wife?"

"She's fine. A difficult, footling breech, birth. The midwife was doing all she could. Only saw this one time before, when I was taking my training. Good thing I remembered what to do."

The farmer hugged Charles. "Thanks, Doc, don't know what we'd do without you. Don't have much to pay."

"Some of those good tomatoes will do."

"You bet. Where ya heading?"

"Richard's"

"You drive safe."

David Huffman

CHAPTER SEVEN

Charles turned onto the dirt road that led to Richard's farm. He hated confrontation. He couldn't make out Richard's tractor in the barnyard. Had he come all this way for nothing?

Driving up to the front of the farmhouse, he saw Richard's wife, Josephine, standing in the front door, wiping her hands on her apron.

Squinting, she cupped her hands over her eyes. "That you, Doc? What brings ya out dis way?"

Josephine, a large, dark-complexioned woman, had tied her long, black hair in a bun. Despite the heat, she had a long dress that covered her knees, but barely her slip. Her scuffed shoes were ankle high. Torn knee-high hose seemed to reach for bottom of her dress.

"Whatya want Doc?" Josephine yelled, as though he a mile away.

"I need to talk with Richard."

"What 'bout?"

"Joe's death."

"Sheriff called a while back. Said he'd be out to talk 'bout things later. It's all over, Doc, far as I'm concerned. Richard, I and the kids need some peace, so we can get on with our lives." Josephine paused. "Cookin' Doc. If ya wanna wait a spell, ya can sit here on the porch, but I gotta go inside for a piece."

Apprehensively, Charles settled on a wobbly straight chair, and gazed to the west. The sun beat down on him. He wiped the sweat from his brow. His heart raced. Beads of sweat again punctuated his forehead. He rubbed his sweaty palms on his pant legs as he contemplated the beautiful summer sky.

It's so tranquil, he thought. Damn, I'm not looking forward to confronting Richard.

He looked to the south just as a dust devil swirled on the crest of the hill. Dust whipped up as the whirlwind moved over the road and spun out into the pasture past a cowherd. That's incredible, he thought, the cows kept grazing, not raising their heads. Like our town, they are oblivious to maelstrom.

He stared back toward the field. A second cloud of dust rose along the horizon. Richard! Charles squinted to make out his tractor as it moved in straight rows, carving the dirt, planting the Milo.

Richard works hard. Farming the land is so basic. Growing food is so essential to life.

Charles reflected on how Richard, a rough ex-marine, had killed before. Somehow, Charles didn't believe he shot Joe. On the other hand, Joe had beaten Richard's daughter many times.

I'd be angry and do everything in my power to stop Joe if I were in Richard's shoes. After all, remembering Richard's comments at the Co-op, when Richard said, a father's gotta do what a father's gotta do. Damn right.

Carrying a jug of lemonade and two tall glasses, Josephine pushed the door open with her foot. "Sorry, don't have no ice, but the water from the cistern is mighty cold."

Charles raised the glass to his lips and drained the bittersweet drink. He smiled at Josephine. "How long before Richard gets done planting?" Charles said, wiping his mouth.

"Could be several hours, can't say."

"Josephine, I'm sorry about all this."

She gazed at him suspiciously. "That all! Ya came out all this way just to say that? Well, you're not half as sorry as we are. I've been sick over what Joe been doin' to Sandy. Glad she don't have to suffer no more."

"Yeah, so am I. But I do need to talk with Richard."

Josephine gave a puzzled look, and then started into the house. Turning back, she said, "Well, Doc, if ya gotta talk wit him, ya need to go out to the field. I'll give ya some lemonade for da both of ya. I know he's real thirsty."

"Thanks."

Charles stopped at the gate to the pasture. A barbwire fence gate blocked his access. He looked in the back seat for gloves, but found only surgical gloves. He pulled at the gate to create some slack. Straining, he lifted the baling wire loop from the post, and the barbwire gate went limp. After kicking the gate out of the way, he drove slowly over the cattle guard. Starting out toward the field, he remembered he hadn't closed the gate. He jumped out of his Jeep, ran back, and secured the gate. He glanced down at his hand. Blood gushed from his finger. For a moment, he didn't feel pain. Then, he felt a sharp jab. "Damn." He applied pressure. Satisfied the bleeding had slowed, he stuck his finger in his mouth and sucked hard to remove any infection.

"You all right, Doc?"

Startled, Charles looked up to see Richard towering over him. Charles stumbled backward. "I didn't hear you come up. You scared me. I can't believe I cut myself."

"Give ya a hand?"

"I'm okay, I think." Charles brushed himself off. "Cut my finger closing the gate. Give me a minute. I'll get a bandage. Don't think I need a stitch."

"Let me help ya, I helped a corpsman once when I was in the Marines. That's a nasty cut."

"Thanks."

"What ya come out all this way for, Doc? Ta helps me plow?"

Charles hesitated, and looked at the tractor. He laughed nervously. "No, I'm not sure I have the time. Or the know-how."

Richard shrugged his shoulders, then he grabbed Charles's black bag and took out some antiseptic. After washing the wound, he wrapped Charles's hand with gauze.

"You're good at that." Charles grimaced as he rubbed his arm with his good hand. "I'm dying of heat stroke. Where can we go to get cooler?"

Richard nodded toward a log down by a cottonwood grove. "I like to sit sometimes to think 'bout things. There's some shade."

They grabbed the lemonade jar, and walked briskly down the fence line to the grove of trees.

After they sat on a log under the cottonwood tree, Richard reached down and grabbed a piece of last year's straw. He twirled the head between his thumb and index finger, and watched as the wheat kernels fell into the palm of his hand. "Last year, the best crop since forty-seven, made nearly thirty bushels, and I gotta good price, too. Did so well, I bought that new tractor. Don't think the harvest'll ever be as good again."

Charles held his glass up to toast the land. He put his glass down, wiped his mouth on his sleeve, and then looked Richard in the eye. "You hear about Joe?"

"Yeah, Sandy called and told Josey and me early this morning. That why ya came out here?"

"In a way." Charles paused to collect his thoughts. "Richard, I gotta ask you something. Did you kill Joe?"

Richard straightened his back and raised his fist. "No, damn it, Doc, didn't kill him. Wish I had, though. He didn't deserve to live for what he did to my daughter. I'm glad he's gone."

Wondering if Richard would attack him, Charles moved down the log to maintain his distance from Richard.

Richard gritted his teeth. "He beat my girl. I tried to talk with her, but she didn't want to leave him. Said she was afraid he'd kill her. I told her she could come live with us, just bring the kids, and come home. She was real afraid of him."

"Why didn't she leave Joe? How could she stay with him after he did all those things to her?"

Richard looked at the ground. "I don't know, I don't know."

"Did you ever try to talk with Joe?"

"Yeah, many times. A mean man and a drunk, I told Joe he had to stop beating on Sandy. Joe denied doing anything. I don't think he remembered when he was sober what he did when he was drunk."

"Where were you last night?"

Richard gaze darted about, then locked on Charles. "I was here with Josephine. You ask her. Earlier, I did go to town. After seeing Sandy and the kids, I went over to the Brass Rail, where Sandy said Joe was drinking. I tried to talk reason into him, but he wouldn't listen. He and Bob were too drunk to get anything through their thick skulls." Richard flexed his arm, showing his Semper Fi tattoo. "Sure, I shook my fist and threatened him. But, I didn't shoot him. I came on home. Josey will tell you that I was home before eleven."

Charles held up his hands. "Okay, okay. One more thing. What were you doing at Joe's Pharmacy this morning?"

Richard's face turned red. "What! You saw me there?"

Charles nodded.

"Sandy called me to tell me Joe was dead. She wanted me to see if he had a will. She's scared, doesn't know how she and her kids will make it."

"I understand."

Richard raised his fist defiantly, his face redder than a sunset. "Damn it, I didn't kill Joe. Can't say I'm sorry he's dead, but I didn't do it."

"Calm down, Richard, we both feels badly about Joe beating on Sandra. After all, we're both family men. I respect that in you. I understand."

Richard softened somewhat. He held his head in his hands for a moment, then looked up. "I tried everything I could, I feel guilty for not stopping Joe."

"So do I." Charles hesitated. He put his hand on Richard's shoulder. "I don't think you killed Joe."

"But he was murdered, wasn't he?"

"I don't know. It looked like he may have killed himself." Charles hesitated for a moment. "I guess we don't really know how Joe died."

As they stood to walk back to the Jeep, Charles marveled at the changing landscape. The sun had slipped behind the grey clouds creating twilight a surreal moment without shadows.

Richard turned. "We gotta work together to solve Joe's murder. I sure hope Sandy didn't do it."

Attempting to look shocked, Charles responded, "What makes you think she killed him?"

"He beat her, didn't he? Maybe she didn't know any other way out of the situation."

Charles knew that he and Richard were on the same wavelength. However, Charles didn't want Richard to know what he knew, or what he had done. "Yeah, I agree. Maybe she didn't know any way out of the situation. For sure, I didn't do anything to stop the beating."

"Yeah, you're right Doc, neither did I."

They walked in silence back to the Jeep to head back to the farmhouse. At the door, Richard reached over and grabbed Charles's shoulder. "I'll tell you one thing, if I find out Sandy killed Joe, I'm never goin' to tell you or anyone else."

Despite a mouth full of cotton, Charles swallowed hard.

"Ya wanna stay for lunch, Doc?"

Charles fumbled as he straightened his bow tie. "No, thanks any way, Josephine. Mary will worry if I don't get back soon."

Charles sauntered to his Jeep. He opened the door, then turned to Richard. "If you're in town tomorrow, give me a call. Are you coming to the picnic?"

"Yeah, we'll be there. Wouldn't want to miss the wheat harvest picnic."

"See you there."

"Okay, Doc. Sure, ya wanna stay for fried chicken? It's my favorite."

"Mine, too. Another time."

Charles headed out of the barnyard and on to the county road as dust whirled behind his Jeep. He strained to see the farmhouse through the rear-view mirror. Richard and Josephine stood on the front porch, only blurs in the fading twilight.

CHAPTER EIGHT

A small brick-front two-bedroom trimmed with green shutters, Barbara's house was similar to the other ranch-style homes on her cul-de-sac. Heat waves rose from the asphalt driveway, making the day appear even warmer, this hot June morning. The children played in their dollhouse in the fenced back yard, unaware of the chaos going on inside the house.

The neighborhood, usually quiet, bustled with the news of Joe's death. Barbara's next-door neighbor had made cookies and a pot of coffee, and had offered to watch the children.

Sandra looked nervously at Barbara as she hung up the phone. "The sheriff wants to talk with us. What'll I say? I don't remember much. God, I wish this would end."

"Don't worry. We'll help you. When does he want to talk with you?"

"Today! He's coming over right now. He wants to go out to my house."

"Why your house?"

"He said he needed to talk with me about last night. Wants to show me something, and ask me questions."

"Sandy, I want to help, but you gotta tell me all you know."

"I don't remember much."

"We talked before about Joe beating you. I know how much you hated him and wanted free of his abuse. You even told me you wished he were dead. I remember you said that."

Sandra munched on a cookie, sipped her coffee, and looked out the window at her children. She turned to Barbara, wiped a tear, and said, "I know I said that, but I just can't remember what happened. You gotta help me. You don't think I killed him, do you?"

"No, I just want you to be careful when you talk with the sheriff. Don't make it sound like you wanted him dead."

Sandra had decided to keep quiet about all she knew, or thought she knew. Anyway, it would be natural if she couldn't remember everything. She knew that people hit on the head often have lapses in memory, and she reasoned that no one would expect her to remember every detail. She struggled to remember what she had told Doc Jamison. She had to keep things straight, and the best way, say as little as possible.

Sandra continued, "I can't remember much, Sis. I remember you coming over to pick up the girls earlier in the evening, before Joe got home. Not much after that."

"Okay, just remember I'm on your side, no matter what."

"Thanks."

They watched the sheriff pull up outside Barbara's house, amble up the front walk, and ring the doorbell.

"Mornin' ladies. How ya doin'?" He looked at Sandra's arm and her face.

Embarrassed, Sandra raised her casted arm and covered her face. She started to reply.

Before she could say anything, he continued. "Bad break. Did Doc set it last night? How many times did Joe hit you?"

"I don't remember. Just remember he twisted my arm, and after that, he hit me in the face with something hard."

"Like the butt of a gun?"

"I don't know. Why do you have to ask me so many questions?"

"It's my job. Sandra, I know Joe hit you before. Wish I could have stopped him, but without your pressing charges, my hands were tied."

She looked at him in disbelief. "What do you mean?"

"I mean that without someone, like yourself, pressing charges against Joe, I couldn't arrest him or get him to stop beating you."

Sandra had mixed feelings. She didn't trust the sheriff, and therefore afraid to tell him the truth about Joe and all the things that had happened. She had difficulty even admitting to herself what had happened. She didn't want to reveal how much she had hated Joe and how she had wanted him dead for a long time.

Barbara wiped Sandra's tears. "C'mon, Sis, grab hold of yourself. Everyone wants to help you."

"You know better, Barbara." Sandra's face grew red with rage. "No one in this town wants to help us. They hate us."

"What do you mean?" Barbara looked nervously at the sheriff.

"I mean this whole town hates us for who we are. They hate us because our great-grandpa, a Negro, staked a tree claim south of Smithville after the fort at Hays closed. A proud buffalo soldier, he thought he had earned the right to settle down wherever he wanted."

The sheriff said, "I don't understand what this has to do with you and Joe."

"Everything. Even though we're nearly white, everyone in Smithville hates us because we are part Negro. They think we're not as good as they are, and that we deserve to be beaten. Because of that, no one would put a stop to Joe beating me."

Sandra looked anxiously at Barbara who looked silently at the floor. Sandra continued. "My mama told me the hate came because of two Negro soldiers who were in great-grandpa's Tenth Calvary Unit at Fort Hays. They killed a white man in the late 1870's."

The sheriff interrupted, "I heard tell of that, but never heard the whole story."

"Momma said that vigilantes from Hays City came and dragged the two Negroes behind trailers, and after beating them, hung them from the Union Pacific Railroad trellises west of Hays. After that, no Negro lived in Hays or Smithville."

"Why?"

"They passed Sunset Laws that prevented any Negro or dark-skin from staying overnight."

The sheriff said, "Yes, but there were Negroes in Ellis. Old Mr. Hill, of Hill City, sold land to the Negroes, called Exodusters, from Tennessee, when they came to Nicodemus up in Graham County."

"That may have been, but no Negroes lived in Smithville. Even though my mama is almost white, she still talks like a Negro and the towns just plain prejudiced against her, and against us."

The sheriff reflected, "Almost as prejudiced as the Protestants are against the Catholics?"

"Yeah, but worse. I think that's why nobody stopped Joe from beating me."

Sandra eyes welled up and she started to cry again. Both the sheriff and Barbara tried to comfort her.

The sheriff said, "Sandra, I'm sorry about all this, but I gotta do my job. I need to have you come with me to your house and answer some questions about last night. There are some things that I need to clear up, and you can help since you're the only one there when Joe died."

Sandra sat in the front seat of Barbara's Scout, as they followed the sheriff west out of town toward her house. They reached the crest of the hill near the Hillman Farm, slowed down, and Sandra looked south.

On a hillside next to the county road, Smithville's cemetery looked ominous to Sandra. A rock fence, made of the same limestone that used to rebuild Smithville, lined the cemetery. Rows of large evergreens marked the perimeter, giving the cemetery a sense of immortality. Most of the graves were marked with large stones, with some dating back to the late 1800s. In contrast, the more recent graves had flat headstones, making the cemetery seem half-empty.

They buried Catholics on the left side of the center road, and Protestants on the right, continuing segregation beyond death. At the end of the driveway, a large grotto stood, marking the Catholic portion of the cemetery. On the far end, Sandra could make out a truck that belonged to Reed's Furniture Store. Reed's two sons were digging Joe's grave for his burial on Monday afternoon.

Sandra wiped her eyes. "I'm glad he's gone. I'm glad my beating is over."

"I know, Sis. I know."

About a mile past the cemetery, the found the Baldwin house. The simple house, with white-painted clapboard siding and shingled roof belied the violence that had occurred within. Joe and Sandra got their water from a well, but their electricity and phones came from Smithville. When they first moved in, they didn't have indoor plumbing, only an outhouse. Two years earlier during a heavy snowstorm, Sandra nearly died when she lost her way trying to get to that outhouse. She would have frozen to death if her father hadn't come over to check on her. After that, her dad put in a septic system and built a bathroom on the side of the house, providing them with indoor plumbing.

Barbara pulled her Scout around the sheriff's patrol car and parked closer to the door.

Sandra fumbled in her purse for her keys, found them, and opened the door. The dank, musty smell of death stopped them in their tracks. Sandra backed up, her knees buckling slightly before Barbara could grab her arm, steady her, and prevent her from falling.

Barbara first guided Sandra to sit at the kitchen table, then she opened the windows to let in fresh air. They sat for a moment, catching their breath before the sheriff spoke. "This won't take long. Just a few questions."

"Okay."

"Sandra. You were sitting here in the kitchen when Joe came home."

"Yes."

"Anyone else with you?"

"Why do you ask?"

"Just answer my questions."

"No, I don't think so."

"No, you don't think so? What do you mean you don't think so?"

"I just can't remember. Joe hit me on the head, and my memory is kinda fuzzy."

The sheriff paused for a moment, as if reflecting on her reply. Then he continued. "I know Joe had been drinking. I talked with Dave at the Brass Rail, and he said Joe and Bob had been drinking there until about eleven last night. They said your dad came and had words with them. Your dad left first, and then Dave said he kicked them out of the bar around twelve. Did you know your dad had been at the bar?"

Sandra looked nervously at Barbara. "No, I didn't. Did you, Barbara?"

"No."

The sheriff continued. "Did you know that Joe had a gun?"

"Yeah, he kept a pistol in his bedside table."

"Did you ever see him shoot it?"

"Sometimes he'd go outside and shoot the gun at the hillside north of the house. I remember he once took shots at a few coyotes. But he never fired the gun inside."

The sheriff walked over to the kitchen door that led into the dining room and closed it, exposing the wall behind the door. He pulled a chair to the wall, and climbed up on the chair, grabbing the door for balance. Reaching up, he stuck his index finger into a hole near the ceiling. Nearly losing his balance, he pulled his finger out of the hole, and turned around to look at Sandra and Barbara.

Pointing at the hole, he said, "Ever see this before? Any idea where this came from?"

"No."

He looked at them skeptically. "This is a bullet hole, and it isn't an old one. I think the bullet hole happened last night."

Sandra stammered. "I don't remember."

The sheriff frowned. "Come with me to the bedroom."

They walked down the long hall. The sheriff pointed to a second hole on the bedroom's ceiling. "How'd that get there?"

Sandra and Barbara kept silent.

The sheriff continued. "I took the pistol back to the office last night and determined that three shots had been fired from that gun, and I think they were all fired here last night." He looked Sandra in the eye, searching for some hint of the effect of his statement. Finding none, he continued. "I also checked the gun for prints, and found two sets. One set, on the gun handle, is clearly Joe's print. The other I can't identify." He paused. "I need to have your prints, Sandra, and yours too, Barbara, to see if either of you matches the other set of prints."

Although Sandra and Barbara sat silently, Sandra fidgeted with her dress.

The sheriff rubbed his forehead. "I gotta headache."

This case is getting too complicated. After I talk with Doc and some others, I'll get back with you. Don't leave town."

"Where would we go?"

"I don't know, just had to say that."

Sandra and Barbara watched out the window as the sheriff drove down the driveway and out onto the highway.

"Sandra, what went on here last night?"

"I don't know, I can't remember."

Barbara looked nervously at the typewriter. The note she had left last night was gone.

David Huffman

CHAPTER NINE

Without a cloud in the sky, the sun's heat poured down as Charles drove into Smithville. Wiping his brow, he thought about his meeting with Richard, and reviewed the events of the past twelve hours. Time wasting, he had to find out who killed Joe.

He glanced at his watch, nearly one o'clock. He looked up at the dashboard and noticed that the gas was gauge nearly empty. He pulled into Paul's Texaco to get gas and call Mary, so she wouldn't worry. Loosening his collar, he stuffed his bow tie into his pocket.

Cupping his hands on his forehead to shield his eyes from the sun, he looked for Paul, finally seeing his friend working on an old Chevy in the lube bay. Charles honked his horn and stood beside his car, expecting Paul to come out and pump gas.

Usually, Charles got full service, but this time, he couldn't wait. He unscrewed the gas cap, and grabbed the nozzle from its cradle. Charles cursed and yelled at Paul for help. Again, no response. Finally, he managed to unwind the hose, and with barely room to spare, he stuffed the nozzle into the gas tank. He squeezed the trigger. Nothing happened. Frustrated, he pulled the nozzle out, then reinserted it. He sniffed the end of the nozzle end and looked down the barrel. No gas. He looked at the dials on the pump. He slapped the side of his head. Stupid me, he thought, I need to reset the pump dial.

As he cranked a handle on the side of the pump, the dials rotated to zero. Pushing a button on the side, the pump started with a whirling sound, and the gas began pumping.

A simple task when your mind isn't preoccupied, he thought. As a kid, he always pumped gas, but how soon one forgets.

His nostrils flared with the nauseous sweet smell of the gas. He watched the nozzle, and listened as the sound of gas hummed down the hose into his tank. He took in a big breath and backed away, staring at the nozzle. It looked like a gun. How ironic, he thought. This gun gives "life" to his car, while Joe's gun took a life. He hoped Sandra hadn't fired that gun last night.

After paying Paul for the gas and laughing about his forgetfulness, he phoned Mary and headed into town. He drove down Main. Usually, there were more people in town on Saturday, but the streets were empty. With the pharmacy closed, there wasn't any place downtown left to get a cold drink on a hot summer day.

He turned on Second and drove past the Brass Rail, where Joe had spent the evening before. The glare of the bright sun blinded him. Charles squinted until his eyes adjusted, so he could see inside. Dave, the bartender, pulled a draft beer for a customer. To Charles, it seemed too early to be serving beer, but saloons weren't his usual hangout.

Charles had been inside the Brass Rail once. That time, nearly two years ago, Dave had called Charles to revive Bob who had fallen drunk off a barstool.

The Rail had six red velvet snooker tables in the front room. The bar with its brass rail adorned the north wall. Budweiser signs blinked on and off behind the bar. In the back room were poker tables.

Poker was illegal in Kansas. In fact, selling beer stronger than 3.2 percent was illegal. To gain notoriety, the Kansas Attorney's General had tried to shut down all gambling and drinking establishments in the state. His antics were particularly unpopular with the VFW. The state police had decided to raid Smithville two years earlier to shut down the games. However, the town had stationed outlooks on Highway 40. When the Attorney's General and his marauders stopped to get gas, Paul and his attendant called ahead, providing enough time for the gamblers to shut down the gambling before the police arrived.

Although the sheriff hadn't been part of the raid that night, everyone in town knew that Sheriff Leiker knew about the gambling. As long as there wasn't any trouble, he let things ride. One time, the sheriff made a mock raid at the bar and arrested two people for gambling. He later let them go with a warning.

Although ambivalent about gambling, Charles enjoyed playing penny poker with friends, but he felt the gambling at the Brass Rail crossed the line. Sitting there, Charles thought back to that night when he came to the bar to help Bob. Mary and he were giving a party when their phone rang. Dave yelled so loud that Charles had to hold the phone a foot away from his ear. The noise in the bar prevented Charles from understanding a word Dave said, only that he had to come over right away. After making apologies to his guests, he dutifully responded. No one expected otherwise.

Charles had found Bob sprawled out on the floor of the bar. He shoved ammonia under Bob's nose. After lifting himself up on one elbow, Bob coughed and gagged, and then proceeded to vomit. Charles jumped back, barely missing the projectile.

"Wanna beer, Doc?" Bob slobbered as he wiped his mouth. "I'm buying, and old Dave will gladly pour ya one."

"No, thanks." Charles covered his face with a handkerchief, pretending to blow his nose, but really wanting to block the stench.

Dave laughed at Bob. "You've already had your limit, Bob. No more credit!"

Although he had heard many stories about Bob, Charles hadn't met him before. Charles knew that Bob and Joe often gambled. They always had some kind of deal going, a surefire way to make a buck. Joe and Bob were always involved in financial deals, but being drunks, they rarely finished what they started. Although they had asked him to invest in their schemes, Charles had avoided getting involved financially with them except for one time when he first moved to town, and then he lost some money. Others in town also hadn't been so wise. Because of many failed business ventures, Joe and Bob had enemies. Charles wondered if one of the victims of their many financial failures had killed Joe to get even.

He wished he could talk with Bob, but Bob was dead. Charles wondered what had been going on between them. What had happened in the bar last night? He started to go inside to talk with Dave, but he needed to get home. He decided to come back later.

CHAPTER TEN

Charles drove up the long tree-lined driveway to his house. Jason's VW was parked alongside Mary's car. Charles got out and walked around the VW, examining the license plates. Missouri tags from the Ozarks. Where in the Ozarks had Jason been? And why the Ozarks?

"Dad?"

Charles squinted into the afternoon sun. Jason, smoking a cigarette, stood on the porch, holding a coffee cup. "Dad, Mom's been worried. Everything all right?"

"I think so. I've been out to see Richard, Sandra's dad, at his farm. Wanted to see if he had any knowledge about Joe's death."

"Did he?"

"I don't know, but I don't think so. For sure, he's glad Joe's not going to beat his daughter anymore."

"So am I."

Charles looked puzzled. "Why do you say that?"

"Sandra and I were friends in high school, remember?"

"Guess I forgot."

Jason's answer puzzled Charles. Remembering Mary's admonition to avoid questioning Jason, Charles decided to pursue the matter later.

"Your mom and I are glad you are home, but we were really hurt when you left without any explanation."

"I know how you feel, but consider my feelings." Jason stirred a large teaspoon of sugar into his coffee. "I resented moving to Smithville." Jason waved his arm, as if pointing to the town. "I didn't want to come here. You took me away from Kansas City. As the high school quarterback, I had won all the games, and really a good player, for God's sake. Everyone said I'd make All State, but then we left, and I never had a chance to finish the season."

"I'll admit you were good."

"You didn't consider my feelings when you decided to move here five years ago. You just came here and we had to come with you. Even Mom said she liked it better in Kansas City."

"Don't drag your mom into this. She understood why we came to Smithville."

Jason continued. "Maybe, but I didn't. After I left two years ago, I wanted to call, but I somehow couldn't. At first, I went to live with friends in the Ozarks. I tried to go to school, but I ran out of money and had to quit."

"You could have called. We'd have sent you money to come home."

"I wanted to be on my own, so I joined a commune with other folks. We lived off the land. I fell in love with the hippie lifestyle. But it got old. Not everyone was honest, or did their part to keep things going. So, I left with my girlfriend, and we went to Kansas City. Been there for the past year."

Charles glanced at his son with a worried look.

"Then this came." Jason reached into his pocket, pulled out a tattered envelope, and handed it to his dad.

Slowly Charles opened the envelope and unfolded the paper. He adjusted his reading glasses and held the letter to the light. "What's this, Jason?"

"It's a draft notice. Three days from now, I have to board a train. If I pass the physical, I'm off to Nam."

"I didn't know. The draft board president promised me he would let me know if your name came up. I guess he forgot." Charles paused. "How did they reach you? No one knew where you were."

"Dad, Uncle Sam always finds you."

"I didn't know."

"Three days, Dad." Jason repeated. "Can you help me, so I don't have to go? You could write a medical excuse about my bad knees."

Charles looked at him in disbelief. "You didn't come here to see us after all. You came here to get me to lie about your health. I don't want you go to war, but for me to lie isn't right." He winced at the irony of that statement.

Mary broke the awkward silence when she backed out of the front door onto the porch, carrying a tray with three cups of steaming coffee. Mary put the tray down on the table, then put her arm around her men. Turning to her son, she said, "Jason, honey, go easy on your dad. He's had a difficult twenty-four hours." With looking worried look, she said, "Jason, you're not in trouble, are you?"

"No, Mom, unless you consider the draft notice trouble. I'm not in any trouble with the law, though."

Charles interrupted. "Let's talk about this tomorrow. Right now, I'm famished. What's for dinner?"

Mary beamed. "Just your favorite fried chicken, mashed potatoes, and corn."

"Sounds great. Let's eat."

They started into the house. Charles grabbed Jason's arm. "I didn't mean to act so negative. I'm glad you're home."

Jason remained quiet.

Mary had set the table with her favorite Depression pottery. Crispy fried chicken, a steaming bowl of mashed potatoes with white gravy, and a bowl of the most beautiful corn on the cob, fresh from their garden, decked out the center of the table.

Charles took in a deep breath, savoring the aroma, then turned to Mary and gave her a peck on her cheek. "Looks wonderful honey. Let's chow down." They grabbed food, as though they were in a boarding house full of hungry people with not enough food for everyone. Jason reached across the table, nearly snatching a drumstick from his dad's hand before chomping down and consuming the meat with one gulp.

Mary beamed. "Somehow, I never thought I'd see you two eating together at my table again."

Jason smiled. "I'm glad to be home, too, Mom."

"Jason, you want to go fishing down at the lake?"

Jason thought for a second. "No. I got plans."

Mary said, "Why don't you go fishing with your dad. It'd be fun and give you a chance to get to know each other better."

Jason replied, "Got other things to do. I'm going out."

Charles straightened his tie, deciding not to confront his son. "At least, let's enjoy some of your mother's fine cooking."

CHAPTER ELEVEN

Even though he had been home less than twenty-four hours, Jason felt cooped up, and had to get out of his parents' house. He drove down Main, turned right on Fifth, and headed toward the high school. There weren't many places to go in Smithville. He decided to go by the high school first, and if he didn't find anyone, he'd go by the swimming pool; beyond that, he didn't know.

Although he had mixed emotions, he wanted to see the old school. School had been difficult for him. The problem for Jason had been living in Smithville. School hadn't been the same challenge that he had experienced when they lived in Shawnee Mission. More than anything, he resented his parents for moving from Overland Park to this podunk town. He had always used the move as the reason he rebelled and ran away after high school graduation, rather than going on to college.

He slowed as he approached the school. He wondered what had happened to his friends. He thought about calling Max and Alex. He wondered about the girls.

He pulled up to the curb in front of the school and got out of his VW. The high school built in 1920 out of the same brick used to pave the streets seemed smaller than he remembered. Behind the school, he noticed a tennis court. Four young kids were hitting tennis balls back and forth. Concealed by the shadow of the building, he looked longingly at them. They were too engaged in their game anyway to notice his intrusion, and that was fine with Jason.

He tried the side door of the school that led into the locker room. Peering through a side window, he could see the basketball court. He rapped on the window. A janitor pushed a mop across the hardwood floor, but Jason couldn't get his attention.

He walked around the back of the school. A gust of hot wind swept around the corner and roughed up his hair. He blinked and rubbed his eyes to clear the irritating dust. He closed his eyes to refocus his mind. Three years earlier, he had been the star of the football team. Each afternoon when the team came up the steps and out on the back lot, there were girls cheering them on and photographers from the <u>Smithville Tribune</u> taking their pictures for the weekly sports section. The reporters would ask questions and take notes, wondering whether the team would be able to win the league title.

One day, he remembered, a reporter intimated that Jason had a chance at making All League and if he did, maybe Jason would get a scholarship to the university. As he thought about that experience, he wondered why he hadn't followed that path so many of his friends took. Instead, he had run away, turned into a hippie and had left all this. He wondered if he could get his life back.

After walking back to the front of the building, he drove down the street. He turned into an alley that headed east of the school. He stopped the VW and, trying to get his bearings, he remembered this alley. After suiting up for football practice every day, the team would run down this alley to the practice field.

He drove down the alley, crossed a small road, and parked next to a gate surrounding the practice field. He shook the lock, but he couldn't open the gate. Frustrated, he looked around, no one in sight. He jumped adeptly over the fence, and walked out onto the field. He found a tackling dummy near the goal post. With clinched fists, he slammed the dummy. He felt a little better. He hit it again and again. Tension lifted a little. Learning to take out his aggression on this field had been more constructive than getting angry at home.

Next to the dummy he found an old football left from practice. After kicking the ball, he decided to pick it up. He tossed the ball with a perfect spiral straight up in the air. Catching the football, he passed it aggressively back and forth between his hands, then he slammed the ball on the ground, nose first. The ball bounced back into his arms. Walking slowly to the center of the field, Jason imagined he was again the star quarterback. He bent his knees holding the ball out with both hands. "Hut one, hut two," he yelled. As though he had taken an imaginary pass from his center, he stepped back, looking to the left, then to the right. He squinted in the twilight, and then he threw the football as hard as he could, as though throwing a winning "Hail-Mary" pass at the end of the championship game.

He listened, but the ball didn't hit the ground. He squinted. At first, he couldn't see anyone, but as his eyes accommodated to the growing darkness, he could see that someone, had caught the football. Out of breath, Jason yelled, "Who's there?"

"Jason, it's me."

He recognized Max's voice. In a way, glad to see his friend. However, he wanted he could be alone so he remained quiet for a moment.

Max said, "I heard you were in town. I came by your house, but your mom said you left in a huff. She didn't know where you went, but in this small damn town, I knew you couldn't be many places."

"How'd you hear that I was back?"

"I don't know, just heard. Why'd you come home?"

"Got drafted. Came home hoping to get my old man to get me off by writing an excuse."

Max said, "Thank God, they've left me alone. Said, because of college, they deferred me.

Good thing, too. My dad couldn't help me even if he wanted to."

Jason looked his friend over. In contrast with Jason and his tie-dyed shirt and scuffed bell-bottoms, Max dressed as if they were still in high school; his hair in a ducktail, rolled-up sleeves highlighting his tight biceps, and crisp pressed jeans rolled up above a new pair of Converse tennis shoes.

Jason resented the fact that while Max had escaped the draft. He knew getting mad at Max wouldn't solve his problem.

Max broke the silence. "Seems to me we need a beer. Wanna hit the Brass Rail?"

Jason replied, "Yeah, I'm thirsty. Take ya on in a game of snooker?"

"You're on. See ya there."

Max had a souped up 1954 Ford with four-barrel carbs and double glass-pack mufflers. Max revved his engine. Then, laying down a strip of rubber in front of Jason's VW, Max sped toward town and the Brass Rail.

"Jeez, slow down," Jason yelled, but Max was long gone. "Whatya trying to do, impress someone?" he muttered under his breath.

Doing his best to keep up, Jason turned right on Main street. Not wanting to fall behind, he floored the gas pedal. The VW groaned as it gathered speed. As the speedometer hit forty miles an hour, a whaling siren and a flashing light approaching him out of the dark quickly halted his exhilaration. "Damn, damn. The last thing I needed was to be picked up by a damn cop." He slowed and pulled over to the curb. He leaned nervously to the right and opened the glove compartment, pushing the disorganized mess around.

"What ya looking for, sonny? Marijuana?"

Jason rolled down his window. "No, no sir. I was trying to find my driver's license."

"Caught ya speeding. Outta the car. And keep your hands where I can see them."

Jason complied. He didn't want a cop to get mad at him. He knew that his clothes and car made the cops suspicious. To stay out of jail, he had learned not to be aggressive with cops: pushing back had gotten him into trouble and caused him to spend several nights in jail. He didn't want that now, so in a quiet, yet noncondescending voice, he said, "Yes sir."

Sheriff Leiker walked around the car. He kicked the tires. He pried off the VW's only remaining hubcap. Jason knew he was looking for pot. He watched nervously as the sheriff shined his flashlight in the back. The light slid over the mattress and up onto the walls, then the sheriff squared off at Jason.

"You new in town?"

Jason stammered. He had to do something to get the cop off his back. "No, I'm Doc Jamison's son. Just here for the weekend."

"For Christ's sake, you sure look different. Wouldn't have recognized you in a thousand years."

"Yeah, that's what everyone says."

The sheriff eyed him suspiciously, then continued his search of the car, but fortunately for Jason, he came up empty. He pointed his light in Jason's eyes. "You been smoking pot, son?"

"No sir."

"Well, your eyes look okay and your speech is clear. I guess you're clean. Gotta give you a warning for speeding, but if I catch you speeding again, I'll throw the book at you."

"Thank you, sir."

"You talk much with your dad?"

"Yeah, we talked last night. He seemed real tired, didn't say much."

"Well, your dad's sure been busy, what with Joe's death, and then Bob this morning."

"Joe?"

"Joe Baldwin. He got himself killed last night. You remember Sandra, don't you?"

Jason said, "Sure, I remember her. What happened?"

"Don't have time now. You be careful now, hear? Where ya going?"

Jason cleared his throat. "Goin' to the Rail to have a beer with friends."

"You old enough?"

Trying to avoid defiance, Jason bit his lip. "I'm 21. That's old enough."

"Guess so. Don't go getting yourself drunk and in a fight. Doc's had enough trouble for one day, and doesn't need you to add more misery." Sheriff Leiker looked menacingly at Jason as he tore the ticket off and shoved it in the window.

Jason parked in the lot behind the Rail, and after locking his VW, walked over to Max's Ford.

Max kicked the side of his car. "What a bummer, getting a ticket."

Jason showed him the ticket. "It's okay, only a warning."

"Yeah, well, that pig won't leave us alone. I'm surprised he didn't get me. Guess he thought he'd take on a hippie for a change. He must've been there when I roared past. I think he's jealous. Bet I could outrun him if he tried to catch me."

"Bet you're right. That rod sounds to me like it's itching for a race."

"Matter of fact, we're having a drag race down by the river road later tonight." Max looked over at Jason's VW. "Doubt you'd be interested in racing tonight."

"Nope, but I'd like to come along. Maybe I could be the starter. I remember how we used to race each night. Will anyone else be there?"

"Most everyone that's in town. Heard tell that some of the girls from high school were going to be there. Most of them have gone on to college at Fort Hays, but they are here for the summer. Plan to have a wiener roast afterward. You're welcome to come."

"I'd like that."

"For now, let's get a beer." They walked into the Rail. Although dark outside, inside, the Brass Rail Jason couldn't see anything. They stood inside the door for a minute to allow their vision to accommodate. Dave stood behind the bar pulling draft for someone.

Jason hadn't been in the Brass Rail before. In high school, the place had been off limits. The football coach threatened any players caught in that place with suspension from the team. He called The Brass Rail a "Den of the Devil." That made coming to the Brass Rail even more enticing. Being inside this place, felt like the ultimate rebellion. The sweet smell of beer mixed with the aroma of smoke waffled out of the room. The lights were low, giving the Rail a sense of mystery.

Pool tables, with low-slung lights barely covering their green velvet, dominated the room. A loud crack sounded and the balls broke, flying toward the corner pockets. Jason sat down on a bar stool, resting his foot up on the rail that gave the place its name, and ordered a beer.

Dave looked at Jason. "Don't remember seeing you before, must be new in town."

For the second time that evening, Jason had to identify himself by reference to his dad.

"So you're Doc's son. I saw him drive by slowly earlier today. Must've had something to do with Joe's death."

Jason quickly changed the subject. "Always wanted to come in here. Do you know that your place is off-limits for the high school?"

"Yeah. But that didn't keep some of your friends from coming in. Don't think they ever got into trouble."

Jason looked at Max, who smiled. "Did you come in here?"

"Several times. Don't think Coach ever really figured it out. A lot of us did. We didn't want to ask you to come with us. Since you were the doc's son, we thought you might tell on us. Anyway, you were kinda difficult to get to know, even though we had great times playing football."

"Wow, I guess I was sort of a loner. I couldn't decide whether to leave Smithville, and kept to myself." "You sure did." Max grabbed his beer. "Let's go. It's getting late, and I don't want to be left out. There's a kid from Ellis that's been talking crap about my car, and telling everyone that he'll race me any time. I told him to meet me at nine. It's almost eight-thirty. Let's get cracking. You can leave your car here and ride with me."

Jason got his coat out of his VW, then locked the front door and checked the back to make sure he locked all the doors.

"Hiding something?"

Jason smiled coyly. "Nothing important, just don't want anyone to steal my stuff."

They drove west of Smithville past the park with the band shell and the picnic area, across Big Creek, and then turned right down a dirt road.

Up ahead, several car lights pierced the dark night.

Max's Ford purred with the growl of his mufflers as he approached the cars. He turned to Jason. "Remember this place?"

"Yeah." Jason had been here a couple times, but not to a drag race.

"We drag on this old highway. It's usually vacant; most people drive on the new highway east of town."

Max got out of the car and pulled up his jeans, and took in a deep breath. There were six cars: five were modified Fords; and one, a fifty-seven Chevy.

Jason felt out of place. In contrast with his hippy attire, everyone else looked the same as Max. Decked out in leather jackets, jeans, and Converse shoes, Jason felt they an anachronism, left from the fifties.

Max reached to his back pocket and pulled out a comb. Then, looking at his reflection in the window, he combed his hair in a perfect ducktail.

Max introduced Jason to the crowd, explaining that they had been friends in high school.

Max turned to the kid from Ellis. "Ready to drag?"

"Let's get it on."

Max slapped Jason on his shoulder. "You stand between me and that jerk, and give us a count down."

Jason stood between the two growling cars that were ready to lurch forward, as though they were hungry wild lions itching to race toward their prey.

Jason looked at the two drivers. "Ready?" They both nodded as they revved their motors to a high pitch. Jason raised a red oil rag over his head. At the top of his lungs, he yelled, "Three, two, one." Then, as he threw the rag on the ground, he screamed, "Go!"

The cars lurched forward, laying a strip of rubber as they gathered speed. Everyone jumped up and down screaming. Caught up in the excitement, Jason, yelled the loudest.

Jason's eyes opened wide. Up ahead, he could see a pair of headlights coming toward the two racing cars. He watched in horror as the two Fords continued to gather speed. Sure they would collide with the oncoming car, Jason panicked, not knowing how to stop them.

The pitch of intensity increased to new heights as each second passed. Jason looked around at the others. No one seemed concerned that the cars were about to crash.

Max suddenly veered to the right, his opponent to the left, and the oncoming car split between them.

Jason slumped to the ground. "Crazy bastards."

One of the girls sat down beside Jason. "What's the matter? They were just playing chicken. Exciting, isn't it?"

Jason shook his head. "That's crazy. Chicken?"

"Yeah, really exciting. It's so boring; we need something to excite us."

Jason shook his head.

CHAPTER TWELVE

Mary shook Charles awake. "Sheriff's on the phone.

There is a terrible accident on the county road east of town.

"Oh my God, Charles exclaimed, "I'm exhausted." Nevertheless, realizing the sheriff needed his help, Charles gathered strength one more time, and sped out onto the county road.

Charles saw lights flashing ahead of him, and car overturned. As he slowed, Charles glanced at the license plate of the overturned car. He sighed with relief as they were from Oklahoma. At least there were no more deaths of Smithville residents tonight, he thought.

"One dead in the car, the other thrown from the car over there," the sheriff yelled and pointed to a girl lying beside the road.

Charles grabbed his bag and ran to the girl. She laid face down, bleeding from her mouth and gasping for air. Charles knelt, took her pulse, and yelled at the top of his lungs to the sheriff, "Help me turn her over. She can't breathe like this."

Gently, he steadied her neck as they turned her slowly onto her back. Charles wiped the blood from her mouth, removing a clot from the back of her throat. She gasped and sucked in a deep breath of air. Her face turned pink. She'd be okay. Charles cleaned her wounds and helped load her into the ambulance. Later, they loaded the dead boy into Reed's hearse.

As the ambulance sped away, the sheriff radioed the hospital in Hays, fifteen miles to the northeast of Smithville. "You do mighty good work, Doc." He paused, then continued, "Thanks for coming out and helping me."

"You're welcome."

"You remember the day you saved my daughter, Doc?"

"Kind of."

"Don't know how you could forget. We'd been fishing at the lake when a bee stung Norma. Wheezing loudly, she obviously couldn't get enough air. I didn't think we'd get to town, so I radioed dispatch. They found you, and you met us halfway, injected epinephrine, and saved her life. I'll be forever grateful. This town is damn lucky to have you and Mary."

Charles looked at the ground. He shuffled his feet and kicked some dirt.

"What's wrong, can't take a compliment? I really mean it."

"I know. Thanks, Sheriff, I'm thinking about something else."

"You hungry, Doc? My boys will clean this mess up. I need a burger."

"Yeah, I guess so. Mary knows I might not be back until early morning. I'm so hyped up, I can't sleep anyway."

The sheriff leaned into his patrol car to pull out his microphone and bark instructions to his deputies. Somewhat intimidated, Charles respected the sheriff. He did his job, and Charles liked that in a man.

Several years ago, a fugitive killed an entire family in eastern Kansas and drove into western Kansas on the run. The sheriff tracked that killer to a culvert south of Richard's farm and cornered him, and arrested the killer without firing a shot. As reported in the <u>Smithville Tribune</u>, the outlaw surrendered to the sheriff after a brief fight.

Leiker locked the murderer in his jail. The town wanted to string the killer up, but the sheriff maintained control. The newspaper ran a second story about how the sheriff protected the town with his bravery. The town gave him a medal. He played it down, though, said that he acted in the line of duty, and that he did what anyone would have done, but everyone in Smithville knew differently.

Charles followed Sheriff Leiker to the Kent Café, an all-night diner on the outskirts of Smithville. Flickering neon lights cast an eerie glow on the red vinyl seats and Formica tables. In the center, a long counter with round stools fronted the grill. A rock-and-roll song blared from a Wurlitzer jukebox at one end of the restaurant. Plates with half-eaten hamburgers, and empty soda glasses cluttered the tables.

The sheriff slid into a clean booth near the back. He yelled at the waitress and ordered a burger, fries, and a cup of coffee. "You hungry, Doc?"

"No, just a cup of coffee."

The sheriff motioned to Guyla, working at the grill. She nodded, and brought them water and coffee.

Charles started, "We gotta talk about last night. Joe beat on Sandra, and she had a broken arm." Charles paused. "When I got there, I found Joe dead."

"Yeah, then you called me. Tell me what you found when you got there."

Charles cleared his throat, hoping to seem nonchalant. "I found Sandra in the kitchen with a broken arm and Joe dead in the bedroom."

"That's what you said last night. You remember anything else?"

Charles started to sweat. Here come the questions, he thought. Should I tell the truth? Charles decided to end his charade and come clean. Sooner or later, the sheriff would find out the truth. If he told him the truth now, maybe the sheriff would go easy on him. He had to take his chances and tell the truth.

Charles's voice quivered. "Things aren't what they seemed last night." He looked the sheriff in his eyes, then glanced away, "I found the 38 at the foot of the bed. I panicked. I assumed Sandra killed Joe, but I didn't know for sure. Guess I'm not sure what happened. Anyway, I didn't want her to suffer anymore, so I changed things to make it look like Joe killed himself."

"Doc, I know Joe didn't kill himself."

"What?" Charles's voice cracked.

The sheriff continued. "Joe was left-handed. You put the gun in his right hand. I didn't know how that happened until now, but it makes sense. I went back to the Baldwin's house this morning looked around and found a suicide note, but I know Joe didn't write it. Joe was a lot of things, but no dummy. The note had the word business misspelled. Joe would never misspell business."

The sheriff paused for a moment, then continued. "In addition, there were three shots fired from Joe's gun. His fingerprints are on the handle, which isn't any surprise since he apparently shot the gun at some varmints in the backyard. I found two sets of prints on the gun. One on the handle, and the second on the barrel."

Sheriff Leiker looked at him. "Doc, you're a good man, but I need to get your fingerprints. Your fingerprints are probably on the gun that is unless you used that handkerchief I found on the floor of the bedroom. I need to confirm that. When we find out whose prints are on the gun, we'll have a better idea what happened. I need to get Sandra's prints, and I need yours."

Charles began to sweat. "Are you going to arrest me for changing the death scene?"

"If that's all you did, I doubt it, but I'll have to think about it. I could charge you with obstructing justice." He looked out the window, then returned his intense gaze to Charles. "Just don't tell anyone else what we've talked about. The fewer people who know about this, the better. For now, I need you to drop over to the office in the morning and give me your fingerprints. I knew someone had changed things, but I didn't know whom. I thought Sandra changed things. I'm actually glad to know you moved the gun."

The sheriff locked his gaze on Charles. "You didn't kill him, did you?"

Charles threw his arms up as if to surrender. "No way, Sheriff, why in the world would I kill Joe?"

"I don't know." He paused for a moment to let Charles sweat. "Actually, I don't think you shot Joe, but I gotta check out all possibilities."

Charles looked anxiously at the sheriff. He wished more than anything that he hadn't moved the gun. Now the unthinkable had happened: he was a suspect.

The sheriff slurped his coffee, then looked at Charles. "If all you did was change the gun around, I think I can overlook that. We all make mistakes. After all, you're too important to this town for me to give you too much grief. Remember the bee sting?" He paused, looking out at the empty highway. "But, I'd sure like to know who killed Joe. What about Richard?"

Charles loosened his grip on the table.

The sheriff continued. "What do you know about Richard? Could he have killed Joe?"

"I drove out to his house today. I don't know, but I don't think he did it either. He certainly had a motive, but he has an alibi,

Josephine." Charles rubbed his unshaven face. "If Richard didn't, who does that leave? Sandra? Her sister? Anyone else who wanted him dead?"

The sheriff poured sugar from the bowl into his coffee. "Just the whole damn town. The way I see it, most of the town had a reason to see Joe dead. A drunk who beat his wife, Joe also had some business deals that went bad. I heard he threatened Bob the other night, demanding Bob pay him back."

Charles stopped suddenly. "Joe threatened Bob?"

"Yeah, I heard tell he threatened Bob. Bob had borrowed money from Joe to pay off a gambling debt, and Joe wanted his money back."

The sheriff cleared his throat. "Doc, there's one more thing I need to speak with you about."

"What's that?"

"Your son."

"What about him?"

"I stopped him earlier tonight. Caught him speeding on Main toward the Brass Rail. That car he's driving is a real piece of junk."

Charles coughed, and, not knowing how to take the sheriff's comments, he stuttered, "He's-he's not in trouble is he?"

"I searched him. I could swear I smelled some marijuana, but couldn't find anything. It's against the law to have that stuff, and I'll bust him if I find any on him."

"I understand. Thanks for telling me."

They looked up to see Guyla standing at the head of their table. "Sheriff, I heard someone squawking on your radio." The sheriff turned on his walkie-talkie and tuned it to the police frequency. A scratchy voice from dispatch told of a disturbance on the other side of town.

Walking to their cars, the sheriff shook Charles's hand. "I'll have to investigate this. I have to finish my report before Monday's coroner's inquest. To do that, I need your report. In order to do that, you have to do an autopsy on Joe in the morning so I can be sure of the cause of death. As for the gun, that's between you and me assuming your prints aren't on the gun."

"You'll trust me to do the autopsy?"

"Yeah, Doc, you're all we got. After tonight, I know you'll tell the truth."

"Thanks for your understanding."

"You help others. I'm glad I can help you."

Charles let out a breath slowly. He pulled out of the parking lot. Heading into town, he couldn't take his mind off the events of the past twenty-four hours. At least, he thought, there probably wouldn't be any legal problems. Despite the reprieve, he felt an inner gnawing feeling, a tenseness that remained. To resolve his own guilt, he had to find forgiveness. He needed to find absolution.

Moreover, he had to talk with Jason. He remembered the sweet smell in the air last night when he first found Jason on the front porch. He knew that sweet smell had been marijuana. Charles had mixed feelings about marijuana, but, for sure, smoking marijuana was illegal, and the last thing Jason needed, in Charles's opinion, was a run-in with the law.

CHAPTER THIRTEEN

Unable to sleep, Mary sipped her third cup of coffee when Charles entered their kitchen.

"Bad wreck?"

"Yeah, two kids were speeding and missed the turn at the bend in the highway east of town. A boy died and a girl nearly expired, but we were able to stabilize her and get her off to the hospital in Hays."

Mary said, "That's a bad curve. Jason told me that he nearly had a wreck there three years ago."

Charles asked, "Where's Jason?"

"He went out with his friends. I tried to get him to stay home, but he wouldn't. I think his friends are more important than we are."

"Now Mary. I'll have a talk with him in the morning." Charles thought about telling Mary about his conversation with the sheriff and the marijuana, but, not wanting to worry his wife, he decided not to get into that tonight.

"Charles, dear," she said, brushing his hair back, "You must be exhausted. I put some clean sheets on our bed, so we can sleep soundly. Hope the phone stays quiet. We both need some rest."

Climbing the stairs, Charles heard music coming from Jason's room. "Damn," he muttered, "Jason forgot to turn off his radio. At least he listens to folk music, not rock-and-roll."

Charles looked in the mirror. He held his eyes wide open revealing his bloodshot whites. He grabbed a washrag, lathered Ivory soap on the rag and rubbed his face. Initially, his movements were slow. Then, they became faster and more forceful, making his cheeks red. After rinsing his face, he stuffed his toothbrush, covered with Crest, in his mouth, and he brushed with such furor that his gums bled, warming the saliva in his mouth. He spat the liquid out hard, splattering the bloody mixture on the back of the porcelain bowl. Embarrassed, he wiped up the mess with a towel, looking around and hoping Mary hadn't seen him.

Although perplexed and ambivalent, Charles felt happy his son was home. Charles didn't understand completely, but there were qualities in Jason that he admired. Jason had a free spirit, a quality that Charles admired, even envied.

In some ways, Charles envied Jason's freedom to be and act as he chose. As the respected doctor, Charles had a reputation to maintain. Everyone expected him to do the right thing. He tried to do his best, but, sometimes, he couldn't meet everyone's expectations. Afraid of failure, he feared making mistakes.

Although he wished he hadn't moved the gun, he had tried to help Sandra. Telling the sheriff the truth had at least made him feel better.

Charles finished in the bathroom, draped his bathrobe on the foot of the bed, and climbed under the covers. He adjusted the pillow, and opened another one of Agatha Christie's books as Mary entered the bedroom. She pulled back the covers on her side of the bed. Humming, she went about the business of getting ready for bed.

She stood behind the closet door and changed into her nightgown. Picking out one of several brushes, she sat on a stool in front of her dresser and loosened her hair slowly.

David Huffman

He watched as her hair fell about her shoulders. She adjusted the mirror and began methodically brushing her hair. The neckline of her nightgown opened ever so slightly, exposing her breast contour. She noticed his gaze, and smiled as Charles took in a deep breath.

Charles closed his book, and looked over the top of his reading glasses. "You're beautiful," he said. He resisted the impulse to run over, grab her by the shoulders, and throw her into bed.

"Love you, too. I'm so happy our boy's home; I've missed him so much."

"So have I."

He arose to walk over behind her and put his hand softly on her shoulder. She put her hand on his and turned to gaze into his eyes. He admired her long black hair punctuated by the gray threads at her temples. As he looked in the mirror, he reached up and touched his own graying hair.

Mary's eyes twinkled as she gazed into his. "Jason's home. I thought I'd never see him again."

Charles replied, "Nor did I. We have so much catching up to do."

"Give him a chance. Don't make him regret his decision to come home. Let's help him feel comfortable." She paused for a moment. "In fact, there's a part of Jason that reminds me of you when we first met when you were in med school. You were an independent back then, just like your son is now. Maybe he inherited that from you. Perhaps that's what makes you feel so uncomfortable."

He pulled his hand off her shoulder, and turned toward the bed.

"I know it's difficult," she said, "But we only have a few days to regain these past years. I'll help."

Charles looked tenderly at Mary. He loved her so. She understood him. If he didn't make it with Jason this time, he might not get another chance. Even if there were another time, Jason might be going to Vietnam and might not come back. Charles dreaded that possibility the most.

In bed, he gave Mary a squeeze. She curled up in his arm and asked about his day.

"There are two things I have to resolve before Jason leaves on Tuesday. I feel in a real bind. I want to tell the truth, but I truly believe the war in Vietnam is wrong, and I don't want our child to die for that cause or any cause for that matter. I agree with those who feel we shouldn't be in Southeast Asia."

"I understand, Charles. What is the other?"

"In a way, they're linked." Charles gathered himself. "The other is Joe's death, and who killed him."

"I told you before I didn't think Joe had the guts to kill himself."

"A lot of people agree with you, but no one knows for sure who did kill him. I'm afraid Sandra may have shot Joe. In a terrible situation, she saw no way out. I've heard about situations where a woman is abused and afraid for her life and feels trapped then decides that the consequences of killing the abusive spouse are less than living with him. That is, if she's capable of deciding anything at that time."

"Charles, tell me the truth, what did happen at Sandra's house last night?"

Charles decided to come clean and tell Mary everything he knew. "When I arrived at the Baldwin house, I found Sandra beaten and bloody with a broken arm. Nearly incoherent, she pointed to the bedroom. There, I found Joe dead of a gunshot to the head." He described Joe and the bedroom, but stopped short of telling Mary everything.

"It must have been horrific."

He paused, picturing the scene in his mind. "You're right. I thought that Sandra had killed Joe. I thought that since she could see no way out of her abuse, she had decided to shoot him and end it once and for all."

"How did you know for sure?"

"I didn't, just assumed, I guess. Anyway, I didn't want her to suffer anymore, so I changed things to make it look like Joe had killed himself. Only thing is I put the gun in his right hand, and Joe is left-handed. Tonight, after the accident, I told the sheriff what I did. I had to come clean."

She looked at him in disbelief. "You changed things. Are you in trouble with the sheriff?"

"I don't think so." The sheriff told me he'd overlook my actions, provided my prints aren't on the gun. I can assure you they aren't. I made sure of that."

"How?"

"I used a handkerchief and for extra protection, I used rubber gloves."

Charles, you were trying to cover up your actions."

"I guess so, just didn't want to get involved. But now I am."

"You risked everything to help Sandra?"

"Are you angry with me?"

"No, I love you for what you tried to do. Does anyone else know?"

"No. The sheriff could charge me with obstruction of justice, but I don't think will. He did make me promise not to tell anyone, so we'll have to keep quiet."

Mary relaxed. "Thank God."

"You're right, honey. Thank God."

Mary said, "Did Sandra kill Joe?"

"I honestly don't know. As I see it, many people had reason to see Joe dead. Sandra certainly had a motive, and so did her father, but he was home with Josephine. Barbara's angry about the abuse of her sister. She had come over that night at some point to get the girls. I just don't know. Others had reason to see Joe dead. Bob and Joe had engaged in some shady business practices that cost Bob a lot of money. They were drinking the night Joe died."

In a quiet voice, Mary replied. "Maybe it would be best left alone."

"It's too late for that."

"How can we convince the sheriff that Joe committed suicide and let things be?"

Charles reflected. "I wish we could. However, we can't. The sheriff knows Joe didn't kill himself."

"I guess you're right."

Charles thought for a moment. "In my opinion, the people of Smithville need to come to grips with their failure to help Sandra. I need to come to grip with my failure to help Sandra. Moreover, I resent the church and that old priest for not allowing Sandra to get out of her marriage to Joe. Sandra feared she would go to hell if she divorced Joe."

Charles caressed Mary's hair.

David Huffman

Mary sat up in bed. "Where do we go from here?"

CHAPTER FOURTEEN

The roaring sound of water penetrated Charles's restless sleep, despite his efforts to block out the ambient sound, by covering his ears with a pillow. Raising his head, he pushed the pillow onto the floor. He looked over, expecting to find Mary still asleep, but she was already up. Rubbing his eyes to clear the sleep, he strained to see the alarm clock. Seven o'clock! My God, I've overslept. Grabbing his terry cloth robe, he staggered into the bathroom.

He splashed cold water in his face, but he couldn't drown the sound of running water coming from the bathroom down the hall. Angry at the lack of hot water, he gritted his teeth and muttered, "Someone's wasting my water."

He punched the intercom. "Mary, you hear that water?"

"Yes, darling, Jason's taking a bath."

Of course, he thought, shaking his head. He wasn't quite used to Jason being home. Besides, he hadn't had a cup of coffee and he had difficulty thinking clearly. What did

Jason do in the shower that took so long? He paused and thought better of his son; at least, he's taking a bath, Charles mused. Maybe he's cutting his hair. Charles could only hope. If Jason cut his hair, it would be a happy day for Charles and for Jason's future.

Charles dressed, and sauntered past Jason's room and down the hallway toward the stairs. Charles shook his head. Clothes were scattered everywhere. Didn't take long for him to trash his room. Just like old times.

Nearing the top of the stairs, Charles heard the sizzling sounds and caught the scent of frying bacon mixed with fresh brewed coffee. His mouth watered. Bounding down the stairs and into the kitchen, he planted a kiss on Mary's cheek. "You're up early."

"Oh, Charles, I couldn't sleep. I'm so glad Jason's home. Hope he doesn't have to leave too soon. I'm worried about the draft notice. Can't you do anything?"

"I can't lie."

"I don't want you to lie, but isn't there something you can do?"

"I'll see. I hope to talk with my friend Robert at either church or the picnic today. Maybe he'll have some ideas on how to help decide about the draft notice."

Mary turned the eggs carefully, keeping the egg yoke from breaking. She said, "Jason awake? Do you know what time he got in? I wish he'd not stay out so late."

"Yeah, he's up and running the shower, using our whole month's quota of water in one bath."

"C'mon, Charles, go easy on him. Don't drive him away."

"I won't. At least he hasn't lost his old habits," he said, giving Mary another kiss.

"Lighten up," Mary chided. "Just be glad he's home. I am. Do you plan to spend some time with Jason before the picnic?"

"Can't right now." He looked out the window, avoiding Mary's eyes.

"What's wrong?"

"I have to go to Reed's and do an autopsy on Joe. The sheriff needs to know what killed him."

"I thought you said someone shot him."

"The sheriff wants confirmation of that before the inquest tomorrow. With the parade and picnic this afternoon, and Church this morning, I won't have time to do the autopsy later, so I thought I'd run down there now and get it done. Shouldn't take long."

Mary looked up from the stove and said, "The sheriff doesn't think you are a suspect, does he?"

"Like I said last night, he told me that he didn't suspect me of the murder. Anyway, why would he let me do the autopsy if he suspected me?"

"I don't know. Just worried."

"Mary, I didn't do anything but try to help Sandra avoid more suffering. I told the sheriff why I changed the position of the gun. He told me that he'd overlook it, assuming nothing else came up."

"There's not anything else, is there Charles?"

"Not that I know of."

Mary relaxed somewhat, and gave him a hesitant smile, then handed him a plate filled with eggs and bacon and an English muffin toasted to perfection. He gulped down his breakfast. After giving Mary a hug, he said,

"I won't be long. I'll call you, if I need any help."

"I hope you won't need my help."

So preoccupied with frying three more eggs and another pound of bacon, Mary didn't hear Jason behind her, and he startled her by grabbing her waist.

"Careful! You'll cause me to burn myself."

"Sorry. Smells great."

He grabbed several pieces of bacon and the three eggs and sat down. "I haven't had such a great breakfast in a long time." He shoved a piece of toast in the egg yellow. "Where's Dad?"

"He's gone to do an autopsy. The sheriff wants him to make sure that Joe died of the gunshot. There's going to be a coroner's inquisition in the morning to decide how Joe died."

"Who's coming to the inquest?"

"I don't know for sure. I guess Sandra, her family, the sheriff, and your dad. Why?"

"Just curious. Who does the sheriff think killed Joe?"

"I don't know."

Jason wiped the last of egg from his plate with his buttered toast. "Where's Dad doing the autopsy?"

"At Reed's mortuary. That's where they take dead people. Why?"

"Just wondered." He gulped down his breakfast, wiped his mouth with a napkin, then, plopping the dishes in the sink, he turned to his mother. "Hey Mom, you got some extra cash for gas? I'm flat broke, and I promised Max and the guys I'd meet them."

She reached for her handbag and pulled out a ten-dollar bill.

He grabbed the money from her hand.

"You don't have to be so quick. At least, you could thank me."

Jason casually replied, "Thanks."

Ignoring his flippant response, Mary continued. "I thought you went out with them last night."

"I did. We stayed out until past midnight drinking beer at the Rail."

"Jason, you didn't get into trouble, did you?"

"No, Mom." With a defiant look on his face, he continued. "Don't push me. I'm a big boy.

I don't have to check in with you every time I do something."

Mary pulled back with an anxious look. "No, I guess you don't. Just indulge me. I worry about you."

"Sorry. I know. I didn't mean to be so sharp."

"Take it easy, Jason. I'm on your side, remember."

Mary didn't understand everything. Her woman's intuition told her to be careful about jumping to conclusions. While happy that Jason was home, she worried about his behavior. He hadn't written for nearly two years, and now he showed up. She knew he didn't want to go to Vietnam, but she sensed something more in the air.

Jason muttered under his breath, "Don't worry, Mom, I'm a big boy. I'll meet you later today. The annual picnic's down at the band shell, isn't it?"

"Yes, there's a parade at one o'clock, and the picnic starts at two. I hoped you'd go to church with us."

Jason stammered. "Oh Mom, I don't do church much anymore."

David Huffman

"I'd like you to see our friends."

"I'll see them at the picnic, remember? Everyone should be there."

"I know, just hoping you'd go to church with us. At least, keep out of trouble." She thought about asking him about his life, and why he'd come home, but Mary didn't like confrontation. She reasoned there would be an opportunity later. She resolved, however, not to let her curiosity run wild. Check out the facts and don't jump to conclusions.

"Don't worry, I will." Jason jumped off the porch and jogged to his VW. He reached inside the window and opened the door with the inside handle. After starting the minibus, he ground the gears as he forced the transmission into reverse. Looking over his right shoulder, he backed down the long driveway and onto the street. He stopped the car, adjusted his rear-view mirror, and looked back at the house. He could see his mom on the porch, waving goodbye. He stuck his arm out the window to wave back. Jason wanted to see Max and the guys; but first, he had other things to do.

CHAPTER FIFTEEN

Charles pulled his Jeep into a parking spot behind Reed's Furniture Store, which also served as the town's mortuary. The building, a two-story structure, had survived the 1930 fire. That's where he'd find Joe's body and probably Bob's, also. Charles loosened his collar and wiped sweat from his brow. Death made him uncomfortable.

Reed's family had always been Smithville's undertakers. Reed's grandfather had been a carpenter, and started the burial business almost fifty years ago; because carpenters built caskets, they chosen to be the morticians. Reed's son enrolled in the mortician school at the university. Reed would therefore be the last of his family his father trained. After his son finished mortician school, he planned to come back to Smithville and open the mortuary on the other side of town.

Charles dug into his pocket and pulled out a key that Reed had given him, and unlocked the door. Slowly, he opened the heavy metal door and peered inside. Nothing moved. All he could hear was silence. Hating to be alone in this place, Charles wished he had asked Mary to come with him.

He walked down a long hall and entered the embalming room. Joe's body, draped with a white cloth, lay on a table in the center of the room. At the end of the room, on a second table, lay Bob's body.

Charles pulled the sheet off Joe's head. Charles cleared his throat, and pulled the cloth down further, exposing Joe's chest, but making sure not to move the sheet below his waist. Charles had seen autopsies at the university, where they examined the body without any sheet covering the body. He didn't feel comfortable then, and he wouldn't feel comfortable now with Joe completely naked.

He carefully examined Joe's grotesque face. The bullet had blown Joe's right eye out of its socket. The bullet's entrance wound had created a bulging hole beneath the right eye, exposing the maxillary sinus. Joe's left eye stared straight ahead disconjugent from his right eye, giving Joe's face a macabre and surreal appearance. Both eyes seemed to bulge out of their sockets, pushed forward by the massive bleeding that had occurred before Joe's heart stopped.

Since Joe had been so drunk, he, unlikely felt any pain. Perhaps out of understanding, Charles winced with pain just looking at him.

Charles put on a pair of gloves and carefully palpated Joe's face. He detected several fractures, particularly in the floor of the right eye's orbit. He stuck his finger in the bullet hole. The bullet track seemed to go up and to the left.

If Joe were left-handed, as the sheriff had said, and Joe had been holding the gun in his left hand, the trajectory of the bullet should have gone up and to the right. Furthermore, if Joe had committed suicide, Charles thought, Joe would have shot himself in the left side of the head or the mouth, but not on the right, as the findings of the autopsy demonstrated. The sheriff had been right, Charles reasoned, there had to be another person involved.

He turned Joe's face aside, revealing a large gaping wound behind the left ear, clearly an exit wound for the bullet. Charles pulled the skin fragments of bone from the wound. He pushed aside the brain tissue looking for the path of the bullet. Some of the brain tissue seemed different in color and texture from the rest of the brain. Could the change in brain appearance be due to bleeding? He felt the abnormal-appearing brain tissue. The tissue felt definitely thicker and more hemorrhagic than the surrounding tissues. Why?

He looked at the rest of Joe's body for anything else unexpected. He examined Joe's abdomen. Nothing abnormal. As he looked up at Joe's chest and neck, he heard a sound that appeared as though something had crashed in the hall outside.

He yelled nervously, "Who's there?"

No reply.

Charles froze, and listened carefully. Quiet. The sheriff said he would come by. Who else could be there? Maybe Reed. No, too early for Reed to be up. Charles wished he had called Reed to help him with the autopsy. Reed had asked Charles to call when he finished, so Reed could embalm Joe for the funeral on Monday morning.

Charles stood frozen for several minutes. He heard no more sounds, so he returned to his task. Even though grotesque, Joe seemed less traumatized than Charles remembered. Certainly things are more sterile here, more clinical.

Charles felt Joe's neck and found a lump just above the collarbone. He palpated the lump carefully. Must be a lymph node, he thought. Charles didn't remember seeing that before. The mass had a firm and gritty feeling. He thought about the strange appearance to Joe's brain, and wondered if these two findings were connected.

He struggled to remain focused. Did Joe have a cancer? He stood back and thought how he'd approach things. It had been a long time since he had performed an autopsy, and he wanted to do his best. He needed to make the right diagnosis. Joe had definitely died of a gunshot wound. But, did he have another illness besides his alcoholism? Did he have a cancer that had spread to his brain?

How would he find out? He needed a needle and syringe to suck some fluid out of the lymph node and the brain tumor. He could look at it under a microscope at his office. He did have some chemicals that he used to stain urine and sputum for determining if his patients had infections. They weren't perfect, like a pathologist would use, but he could get some information by staining the fluid, and perhaps he would find a clue to Joe's condition.

He took off his gloves and grabbed the phone from the wall. Mary picked up after the fourth ring. "Honey, I found something really strange on Joe, and I need your help."

Mary replied nervously, "What kind of help?"

"I need you to go by the office and get me my black bag and three or four glass syringes with two eighteen gauge needles, and bring them here, so I can take some tissue samples from Joe's body."

"What do you need that for, Charles? You know how I hate that place."

"Please, I know how difficult it is for you. But please, I need your help and I don't want to leave here."

"Why?"

"I can't leave Joe's body right now. Besides, I think someone's watching me. I heard a sound from the hallway."

"What do you mean you heard a sound?"

"Probably nothing, please bring me the syringes. I don't want to leave here."

Mary reluctantly agreed, saying she'd call from the office if she couldn't find what he wanted.

Charles wished he had paid more attention to pathology in medical school. Paul Jacobs had been one of his best friends at the medical school and, if Charles remembered correctly, Paul worked as the senior pathologist and head of the pathology department at the university. When he finished with the specimens, he'd call Paul to discuss his findings. If Paul could help him, Charles would send him samples in formalin, for preservation, on the evening train. The samples would get there by the morning, and he might have a definite answer before the inquest tomorrow afternoon.

If Joe had a cancer that had spread to his brain, what difference would it make? His alcoholism and beating Sandra were paramount and the tumor, if it existed, didn't get him shot. The cancer might explain Joe's rage and aggressive behavior these past few months. Would knowing that her husband had cancer make Sandra feel differently about him? He didn't know.

How would the town deal with it if Joe did have a malignancy? Could a cancer explain his behavior, and mitigate the seriousness of his drinking and aggressive behavior?

A sound of a door slamming shut startled him. Remembering the crashing sound he had heard earlier, Charles realized someone had been in the building and probably watching him. He wiped his hands on his white coat, walked cautiously to the door, and opened it. He looked up and down the hall. He saw no one. He shook his head, wondering if he imagined the sounds. He took in a deep breath. In the air, he smelled a sweet scent. Perfume? Could the smell be marijuana? He called out for Jason. No response.

"Anybody here?"

No response.

Charles walked down the hall, and opened the back door into the alley. Only his car sat in the alley.

He turned to walk back into the building and ran into the sheriff, standing in the middle of the hallway.

Charles said, "You been here long?"

"No, just got here. Came in the front door."

"Did you see anyone?"

"No, why?"

"I think someone else is here."

"You're too jumpy, Doc. Didn't see or hear anyone else."

Charles inhaled a deep breath to get a whiff of the sheriff's after-shave, but that smell was distinctly different from the earlier smell. He wondered if Jason had been there. The sweet smell he had experienced earlier reminded him of the scent he smelled the night Jason showed up on his porch.

The two men returned to the morgue, and Charles went over his findings. "Joe died of a gunshot wound all right, but the route trajectory isn't compatible with a suicide. I know I moved the gun while trying to make it look like a suicide. But you're right, he couldn't have killed himself." Charles put on his gloves again, and demonstrated for the sheriff. "The bullet trajectory through the skull is wrong for him to have shot himself. If he had shot himself, he would have put the gun in his mouth, or to the left side of his head that is assuming you are telling me the truth, Sheriff, that Joe was left-handed."

The sheriff pulled Joe's military record from his pocket. "Look here. Says Joe's left-handed."

Charles read the report, and nodded. "I also found a surprise. Sheriff, I think Joe had a cancer."

"How you figure that?"

Charles pointed out the mass in Joe's neck and the area in the brain that looked different from the rest of the brain tissue.

"Couldn't that area in the brain be distorted by the gunshot?"

"Maybe. I'm going to send specimens to my friend at the medical school. He can help clear things up. Maybe it had something to do with Joe's meanness, him hurting Sandra and all. Maybe he drank alcohol to kill the pain in his head." Charles looked back at Joe's body. "He had to have had some pain, though not as much as when he got shot."

"I don't care what else you find, Doc, he died of the gunshot, didn't he?"

"Yeah."

"Let's don't lose sight of that. For now, let's keep this cancer thing between you and me. It may come up in the hearing tomorrow, but I don't want it to confuse the central cause of his death. Okay?"

"Okay. The cancer could help explain Joe's behavior. If Joe had a brain cancer, it could totally change the way we approach the case. Maybe Joe wasn't responsible for his actions. Maybe he drank to dull the pain. When he got drunk Joe changed, but more than that, lately I've noticed changes in his personality when sober. Guess I thought the alcohol pickled his brain."

The sheriff rubbed his chin. "So did I. I don't want to ignore this, just don't know where it fits in yet. In my opinion, the fewer people that know about this right now, the better."

"Your call. You're in charge."

"Right. You can go ahead and send the stuff to the university. Will it cost anything?"

Charles shook his head. "I'll pay for it. It's on me."

"Well, keep track of things anyway. Let's not close any doors, okay?"

"Sure."

The sheriff, needing to complete his paper work, headed back to his office. Charles continued to examine Joe's body until Mary arrived with the syringe and needle.

When Mary knocked, Charles opened the door and motioned for her to come in.

She stood her ground.

"Come on, Mary, I need the syringes and needles."

She hesitated. "I don't want to come in there. You come here and get your syringes."

Charles took the syringes, then asked, "Where's Jason?"

"He went to visit his friends. I tried to get him to come to church, but he refused."

"You can wait outside in the car if you don't want to come inside. I'll get done as soon as I can."

Returning to the table, Charles took a bottle of lidocaine, a numbing agent, from his black bag and drew a syringe of the liquid. About to inject the contents of the syringe into Joe's neck, Charles stopped and put the syringe down, and then slapped the side of his head. Stupid me, he thought, Joe's dead, and he can't feel a thing I do to him. Charles glanced around, hoping no one saw his behavior. He picked up a 20 cc syringe. After fitting a needle to the syringe, he plunged the needle deftly into the mass in Joe's neck, and sucked back bloody fluid. He put a second needle into the brain tissue and sampled the abnormal-looking tissue. Then, for comparison, he took a sample of Joe's normal brain tissue.

Charles gave Joe a last examination to make sure that he hadn't missed anything. Satisfied, he put the syringes in a box. After washing his hands, he covered Joe with a clean sheet. He wanted to replace the bone fragments and make Joe's face less distorted, but realized that was Reed's job. He picked up the phone and called Reed to tell him that he could finish embalming Joe's body for the funeral.

Before leaving the room, Charles stared at Bob's body. Charles realized he had been so preoccupied with Joe he had forgotten about Bob. Charles wondered if he should autopsy Bob, as well. Looking at his watch, he realized that if he did he would be late for church and the picnic; and he knew he couldn't miss church. For one thing, Mary wouldn't understand, and for another, he needed absolution.

After all, Bob had died after complaining of severe abdominal pain and after vomiting a large amount of blood. Charles reasoned that a bleeding ulcer, aggravated by alcohol, had caused Bob's death. That would be sufficient for the death certificate.

As he started out of the room, he remembered the black smudge he had seen on Bob's hand earlier in the day. He lifted his hand and examined it carefully. The black mark gone, Charles realized that Reed had washed his body removing all traces of the black mark. If that black mark had been gunshot powder residue, the opportunity to implicate Bob in Joe's death had been lost.

Without speaking a word, Charles and Mary drove onto Main, past Joe's Pharmacy and the courthouse to Charles's office. Mary waited in the front room, while Charles stained the tissue and examined the slides under his microscope. He looked up, rubbed his eyes, and peered out the window, taking in a deep breath. He couldn't be certain, but the cells looked malignant to him. He'd have to wait for confirmation from his friend at the university. After reviewing the slides again, he squirted the remaining fluid into a jar filled with formalin. He carefully packaged the specimens in a box, and they walked briskly to his Jeep.

They drove to the train depot, and gave the samples to the conductor for shipment on the afternoon train. In twelve hours, the specimen would be in Paul's hands. With luck, Paul would call Charles in the morning with the answer before the coroner's inquest.

Charles washed up in the station restroom and changed into the clean shirt and bow tie that Mary had brought for him.

Mary admired him as he got back into the car. "How's my handsome husband? You okay, Charles?"

"Yeah, I'm okay. Just a bit frazzled."

He turned the rear-view mirror toward him, and brushed his hair with his fingers. After readjusting the mirror, he drove out of the parking lot and headed down Elm Street toward the First Methodist Church and the Sunday service.

As they turned the corner, the church bells announcing the ten-o'clock service greeted them. The First Methodist Church dominated the block at the corner of First and Elm streets. Like Reed's Furniture and Mortuary and the high school, the church had escaped the fire, and it still had its original wooden frame structure. Above the front steps, a large steeple, containing bells, created a magnificent façade. Inside the double front door, ushers and greeters stood at attention in the narthex that led into the sanctuary. On either side of the center aisle were long hardwood pews. Charles had tried to donate pads for the seats, but the minister had resisted, feeling that the parishioners might fall asleep if they became too comfortable; he right, in Charles's opinion.

Mary and Charles found their usual place on the right side about halfway down. In front of them, a wooden pocket contained a fan, a pencil, and cards for people to sign if they were new to the church. Since no one had moved to Smithville during the past two years, Charles wondered why the church kept the cards in the pews.

Mary waved the fan in an effort to get cool by moving as much of the stifling air as she could. Although they could hear people talking outside the church, and except for an occasional cough or someone clearing their throat, silence filled the church.

At exactly ten, Mrs. Schneider opened a door behind the pulpit and, with a flurry, sat on the organ bench. Under her weight, the bench creaked, as though complaining. She raised her hands then hit the keys with "Nearer My Lord to Thee," and the service started. The choir had the summer off, so Mrs. Schneider belted out a solo. Her whiny voice did have some skill, but Charles winced as she hit the high notes.

David Huffman

Pastor McCurty read scriptures about Jonah and the Whale, then proceeded to give a sermon for twenty long minutes about the relevance of that story. Charles wished he had had the courage to tell Mary that he had other things to do besides go to church. He couldn't see the relevance of Jonah to what he had been through for the past thirty-six hours, unless the circumstances of Joe's death were the whale and he Jonah.

On the first Sunday of the month, he had to endure communion. Charles didn't look forward to taking communion: Methodists used grape juice; at least Catholics had wine.

Charles thought back to four years earlier, when Sunday school teacher asked him to sign a temperance pledge and promise not to drink alcohol. Jason had refused. That had been Jason's first act of rebellion. Charles, Mary, and Jason had had to meet with the pastor that night. Jason argued that he didn't have to sign anything. Besides, signing a pledge at his age didn't obligate him for behavior later in his life, although, in fact, that the purpose of having the youth of the church sign the pledge. However, Jason had been right not to sign the pledge, in Charles's opinion. Even though they were proud of Jason for his strong will, Jason's behavior embarrassed them.

A cool glass of grape juice placed in his hand by the minister interrupted his thoughts and brought Charles back to the present. He took the glass dutifully, drank the juice, and bowed to the pastor.

After church, Charles and Mary thanked the pastor and said their goodbyes, for they had to hurry home and get ready for the parade and the annual picnic.

CHAPTER SIXTEEN

As they drove down Main Street toward home, Charles thought about the past thirty-six hours. He didn't know who killed Joe. He remained worried that Sandra had shot Joe. He could almost hear the town gossip, speculating who killed Joe. Certainly, everyone had his or her theories. In a way, though, the town had been uncomfortable with Joe's alcoholism, and embarrassed for not stopping Sandra's abuse. Charles knew that most Sandra, indeed the whole town, felt liberated by Joe's death. In a way, Charles felt glad also though he sensed guilt for that thought.

Charles needed equanimity. He looked forward to today. Smithville celebrated the wheat harvest every year at this time. Nestled in the heart of Kansas, this conservative town had re-elected Eisenhower by a landslide. Charles hoped to win Mary's carrot cake. Until then, he wanted to read his new book, <u>The Maltese Falcon</u>.

He sat down in his library, and opened the book. Before he could get past the first page, Mary interrupted him.

"Charles, you'd better get crackin' and churn the ice cream for the picnic. I used extra rich fresh cream, eggs, and big red strawberries from the garden. You need to get started right away. If you don't, we'll miss the picnic."

Charles put down his book reluctantly, and took the silver crock filled with ice cream mix, from the refrigerator. Looking to see if Mary was watching, he unscrewed the lid quietly, and scooped a big glob with his finger and spooned the slurry into his mouth.

"Charles, cut that out. We won't have any ice cream if you eat the mix before it freezes."

He swallowed so fast, his head hurt. "Darn, I thought you wouldn't catch me."

Mary chided. "Go on, little boy, and churn the ice cream."

He got great relief from the simple task of making ice cream. With the silver pot secure in the bucket, he layered ice and salt around the inside of the wooden container. After connecting the shaft to the silver pot, he sat down beside the bucket. At first, he turned the crank with ease. As the ice cream set up, rotating the crank became harder. He stopped, rubbed his muscles, and stretched his hand, opening his fingers wide to get rid of cramps. When he could no longer turn the crank, he released the lever. Covering the wooden ice bucket with a burlap bag, he lifted the ice cream container into the back of his Jeep.

Before the picnic, they were going to the annual parade. Charles felt they could see the parade best from the porch of his office. After parking his Jeep behind his office, they walked around the side of the building to the front steps. A crowd had already gathered in an ideal place, in front of Charles's office, that had a large cottonwood to shade them from the summer heat. From here, everyone could see the parade as it turned the corner and headed east on Main toward the railroad depot.

The parade initiated the Summer Solstice Festival to celebrate the wheat harvest. After the annual picnic in the city park, the festivities would end with a dance at the VFW Hall. Most of the farmers thought the celebration should wait until after the harvest. After all, hail or drenching rains could still hurt the crop, but the tradition had started many years ago, and like many other things, change came slowly to Smithville.

Charles brushed dust from the folding chairs, and handed one to Mary.

"You expect me to sit on your old fishing chair?"

"You don't have to, but I thought it'd be better than sitting on the curb. Suit yourself."

She took the chair, but before sitting, she wiped it again with her handkerchief.

Charles chuckled. "Unlike some of the dirt that people have gotten into, this dirt will h off."

Mary grinned. "You're right. Sometimes the parade is really long, and I need to rest my weary legs."

Their view obstructed, Charles moved to the curb. As it turned out, Gertrude had saved them a spot. "After all," she proclaimed as she moved people aside, "It's your office,

David Huffman

Doc, and you deserve a good place to see the parade."

The summer sun was high in the sky, and despite the partial cover of the cottonwood tree, everyone was sweating profusely. In the distance, they could hear the band playing a Souza march.

"Here they come."

Everyone stood as the honor guard of Boy Scouts presented the colors to the community.

An old man, too tired to march in the parade, stood at attention in his tattered World War I uniform and saluted the American flag as it passed.

A horse-drawn wagon followed, and contained five beautiful girls dressed in formal gowns. Charles recalled the year when Sandra had been in the queen's entourage. How her life had changed.

After the queen's float, a rag-tag group of soldiers from previous wars marched, holding their heads high. Smithville had only two soldiers left from World War I that could march in the parade. Although there were a few who had fought in Korea, the majority of the soldiers were from World War II. The World War II vets seemed the most proud.

Charles looked carefully at the marching soldiers for young men, but there were none from Vietnam. Charles wondered why, until he remembered that only two of Smithville's young men had gone to Vietnam; both were dead and buried in the cemetery.

Panic hit Charles. Jason could go to Vietnam, and die. Smithville was a patriotic town, but he didn't want his son to die in that war, particularly since, in his opinion, the war wasn't right. He had to talk with someone.

Although the veterans had passed, Charles remained standing. Mary pulled at his coat. "You all right?"

Charles gathered himself. "I'm okay. Just lost in thought."

"What about?"

"Jason. Jason and that damn war."

"I know honey. Let's talk about it later. Try to enjoy the parade."

Following the veterans there several horses, an old Model T Ford, and finally, Richard's combine.

Richard sat proudly on his tractor pulling his antique combine, waving to the crowd. Charles knew that Richard, with all his experience from World War II, would know what to do about Jason. Charles decided that he'd talk with Richard.

He watched attentively as Richard's tractor approached their vantage point. Richard owned several antique combines that he had restored. Charles wondered whether the old workhorse could still thrash wheat.

Richard's thrashing machine reminded Charles of the one he worked on as a young boy. In 1935, Charles went Fort Hays College. He needed money, so he worked that summer for twenty-five dollars a month helping his dad and uncle cut wheat for their neighbors. Dirt poor, Charles relied on that summer's work for him to pay for college tuition. Once he started school, he won scholarships, and continued working his way through medical school. Charles longed for those simpler times.

With lights flashing and siren's blasting, Smithville's fire engine and the sheriff in his patrol car heralded the end of the parade.

Everyone stood and saluted the officers before folding their chairs and heading toward the picnic.

Charles and Mary drove out the back alley behind his office and turned left on Sixth Street before heading west on Elm Street. The midday sun bore down, and sweat poured from their foreheads. As Mary fanned with a newspaper, she reached inside her dress and straightened her bra strap. "Sure hope the ice cream doesn't melt." She gave him a tender look as she reached over and held his hand. She slowly placed his hand on her thigh.

"Stop that, you'll get me excited and cause an accident."

Mary blushed as she squirmed and moved away from Charles toward the door.

"Why'd you do that?"

Mary stammered, "Oh Charles, we're not too old, are we?"

"Not in my opinion." He winked.

Mary's face reddened. "Nor in mine."

Charles stopped the car and pulled Mary gently toward him. He caressed her cheek, and gave her a big hug.

Mary quivered. "Not now Charles, later. We must hurry, or we'll be late."

Charles beamed. Excited as a young man on his first date, he floored the gas pedal and sped toward the park.

A banner covered the entrance: WELCOME TO SMITHVILLE'S SUMMER PICNIC. The screeching tones of the junior high jazz band murdering "Count Basie" emanated from the band shelter at the far end of the park.

Rather than breaking into applause, Mary clapped her hands over her ears. "They're really bad," she complained. "They need to either tune their horns or practice more."

Charles agreed. "The high school band will be much better."

"They should be."

Charles wheeled around to greet a friend. "Robert, I'm glad you're back. Didn't you go to Colorado?"

"Yeah, I left to escape the heat, but I'm back. I didn't want to miss the summer picnic."

Robert Applebee, the high school principal, was highly respected. He and Charles were good friends. In addition to teaching, Robert regularly read scripture at Saint Paul's Catholic mass. Tall and lanky, like Charles, Robert usually dressed in a suit and a bow tie. Although more casual today, he still wore a buttoned-down shirt.

They embraced, patting each other on the back. Charles beamed. "Good to see you, Robert. It's been a rough two days."

"That's what I understand. What can you tell me?"

"Not now." Charles grimaced. "Help me unload the ice cream and cake." He wiped his forehead. "Sure is a scorcher."

"That it is."

They unloaded their cars, and carried the picnic baskets and ice cream to a table near a large cottonwood. The ladies spread a red-checkered cloth over the table, while the men got rocks to hold down the corners. Mouth-watering smells of fried chicken, gravy, and delightful carrot cake replaced the scent of cottonwood.

They wore straw hats trimmed with Bob Dole's name in red, white, and blue. A World War II veteran from Russell and a new politician, everyone anticipated a great future for Bob

Dole. The sounds of summer were everywhere. Squeals rose from the swimming pool. Loud shouts from the volleyball game replaced roars of a softball game in full swing emanating at the other end of the park. Everyone appreciated the scattered cumulus clouds that provided occasional protection from the sun's bake.

Before eating, Mary asked Robert to say the blessing. Everyone held hands, and bowed their heads.

Robert began, "Lord, bless this food to our bodies and us to Thy service. Bless our town. Protect us from evil, and forgive us our sins." He paused a moment and looked around the table to see if anyone had opened his eyes. Bowing his head again, Robert continued, "Protect the wheat harvest from hail and damage, and bring us peace. Amen."

Everyone responded with a loud amen.

For a moment, all the turmoil of the past two days seemed to fade. With his family and friends, the day seemed beautiful and the food looked sumptuous.

Charles moved over, so Jason could sit down between him and Mary. He squeezed Jason's hand. "I'm glad you're home son."

Everyone grabbed the bowl of food nearest to him or her, and after helping themselves, passed the food in all directions until every plate contained a heaping high portion of fried chicken, corn on the cob, potato salad, and baked beans. No one would go hungry today.

When they couldn't eat anymore, Robert grabbed Charles's arm. "Come on, while the ladies clean up, and let's play softball."

Charles begged off. "Forgot my mitt."

"You're not getting off that easy. I have two."

"Oh, okay, but I'm kind of rusty. It's been a long time."

They grabbed the ball and mitts, and walked down the path toward the field. "What's your best position, Charles?" Robert yelled. "I always wanted to pitch."

"Catcher, I guess, though I usually played right field."

"You, too? I thought I was the only one bad enough to play right field every time."

"Well, me too. Usually, the team picked me last. No one ever hit a ball into right field. I think they reasoned that I wouldn't embarrass the team, if they stuck me out there."

The men chose teams, while the women watched. Charles and Robert laughed as they ran onto the field. They enjoyed themselves. There were no high stakes. Both Charles and Robert batted, but neither got a hit.

They returned to the table, and Charles patted his belly and turned to Mary. "I'm really stuffed from such a fine dinner, honey. Only one thing more that I need." He turned and looked at a long table filled with cakes. "As for me, I'm going to win that carrot cake you made, Mary. I can't let anyone else win my favorite cake."

To win a cake, everyone had to participate in a game of musical chairs. They all stood behind a circle of chairs. When the music started, the hopefuls walked slowly around the chairs, watching one another, while keeping their hands on a chair. Suddenly, the music stopped, and everyone found a chair but

Robert. Charles laughed, pointing a finger at his friend. "Better luck next time."

As the music started for the second round, he felt Mary tug at his sleeve. "Charles, Sandra is out of control, yelling and carrying on!"

"Oh no! Not now! I have a chance to win. Go get the sheriff. Let him deal with Sandra."

Mary replied, "You know you're the only one she'll listen to."

Thus, he acquiesced and followed Mary to the other end of the band shell.

Charles nervously surveyed the growing crowd. He had no difficulty finding Sandra and her parents. A large crowd had gathered to watch the growing confrontation.

Charles approached cautiously. "Sandra, you okay?"

Sandra looked up. "No, Doc, I'm not okay. I'm really mad, mad at this whole damn town."

Sandra's black-and-blue eyes glared at the gathering crowd. Josephine reached out to Sandra, but she pulled away. "Don't patronize me. Some things I gotta say and you all need to hear me out."

Everyone cringed. "None of us want confrontation, Sandra," someone said. "This isn't the right place, not here at the picnic, when we are having fun."

"I don't care what you want." Sandra raised her casted arm in clear view. "My life has been horrible. None of you had to live with Joe. None of you had to put up with his drinking." She began crying. "I couldn't sleep at night. He-he threatened to kill us."

She paused, looked away, and then she glared at the crowd. "I thought about killin' him."

Charles shook his head. "Tell me you didn't."

Sandra cried. "You know me better, Doc." She dropped her head. "I could never kill Joe. I hated my life, but I'd never kill him."

Richard said, "Sandra, we're sorry, but no one knew what to do. We knew Joe beat you. We wanted you to leave him and come home."

Sandra stiffened. "I couldn't do that. I didn't think anyone heard my cries, or cared."

Richard held his daughter. "I love you. Please, don't be angry." He paused. "We are all to blame for what happened, even you."

Stunned, Sandra pulled away. "What do you mean? Joe's my fault?"

"In a way, we've all failed. Tell her what you told me, Doc."

Charles began. "I went to a meeting in Kansas City not long ago. They discussed some new ideas about how to help alcoholics. Family and friends of an alcoholic are in some ways as responsible for the drinking as the alcoholic. To break the cycle, everyone has to quit playing games. Wives must stop covering up, and friends need to stop making excuses. We all could have done better."

Silence, as stifling as the heat, engulfed the crowd.

Sandra dried her eyes. "I'm sorry. I know it sounds horrible, but I'm so relieved to go home without fear." She started crying again.

Charles hugged Sandra until she stopped sobbing.

Jason, who had been standing in the back of the crowd, came forward and put his arms around Sandra. She wiped her face and smiled.

Jason said, "You okay?"

"I-I think so."

The crowd dispersed, and Jason helped Sandra sit on the park bench.

Charles headed back to the cakewalk and bumped into Jean Applebee, carrying Mary's carrot cake.

"Give you twenty dollars for that cake."

"Not on your life, Charles. Your wife's cakes are the best. Won't sell it."

"I'll trade you some strawberry ice cream."

"Won't work, Charles. Outta my way."

Dejected, Charles cleared the picnic table.

After loading the Jeep, he helped Mary into the front seat. "I love you, Doctor Jamison." Mary smiled coyly. "When we get home I'll fix some lemonade, and make you another carrot cake."

"I'd really like that," he sighed.

They sat in the car, admiring the evening sun as it fell into the horizon creating a yellow hue of twilight. Mary scooted toward him. As she put her head on his shoulder, Charles put his arm on hers and gently squeezed his beloved.

Charles noticed Jason and Sandra sitting on a bench at the far end of the park. He turned to Mary. "What do you think they are talking about?"

"I don't know. I'm glad he's taking an interest in our town, though. Sandra needs a friend, someone who can listen to her and support her."

"I understand, I think. Just wondered."

"Charles, tell me again what happened Friday night?"

He took his hand off her shoulder, and told her again about the night and finding Joe and Sandra and helping set her fractures.

She turned around. "Look me in the eye. I need to see your eyes."

Charles looked at his feet, then up into the cottonwood tree.

"Charles, look at me. You're not telling me everything. I can't help you if you keep secrets."

He cleared his throat. "Not now, not here." He looked over at the crowd. "Let's take a walk."

They got out of the car and walked along the dike, down into a grove of trees east of Big Creek. In the center of the park, they found a picnic shelter. Built of the same limestone that the town used to rebuild after the fire in 1930, the shelter was a popular place for a picnic. They sat on the bench near a fireplace that contained glowing embers.

He looked around for water to drown the embers. Finding none, he closed the grate to cover the coals, to prevent the sparks from escaping, and start a fire in the cottonwoods. Satisfied he had controlled the fire, he looked at Mary for approval.

Mary watched him. "Always taking care of things."

"Does that upset you?"

"No. Just admiring you and your thoroughness. Some might accuse you of avoiding the subject. But not me."

"Mary, this is very hard, but what I did Friday night—that wasn't right."

"At the Baldwin's?"

"Yes."

Charles cleared his throat, and fidgeted with his bow tie. "I felt so guilty about not stopping Sandra's abuse."

Mary scooted closer to Charles, and put her arm around him. "I understand you thought you were helping Sandra. But maybe Sandra didn't shoot Joe. Maybe Richard shot him, or maybe Bob. God knows Joe had many enemies in our town. Any one of them could have killed him. He had enough people who hated him for his behavior, and most importantly, many lost their money in his schemes."

"Even we lost some money."

"I know, Charles."

"This morning, when I did the autopsy, I didn't say anything to you, but I think Joe had a brain cancer. The sheriff asked me to keep it a secret, but I have to tell you. I need you to help me and provide advice for me. That's what I took to mail to Paul at the medical center. I should know for sure later today."

"I'm confused, what does that have to do with Joe getting shot?"

"If he had a brain tumor, it might explain why he drank so much, and explain his crazy behavior. It might even explain why he hit Sandra. No excuse, mind you, but it might help explain things. Knowing that he had a brain tumor doesn't help me understand how he died, or who killed him. I still think it might have been Sandra. Alternatively, possibly Bob, or God knows anyone could have shot Joe. At least, I know it wasn't me."

He hugged her. They sat quietly, looking toward the setting sun.

In the distance, a lone hawk rode the updraft of the heat convection that emanated from the limestone cliffs. Unseen in the grass, a mouse scurried from its hole to get food. The hawk had been patient. Suddenly, the hawk plunged into the tall grass. A puff of dust covered the ground. A moment later, the hawk climbed out of the cloud carrying her prey, the unsuspecting mouse, to the hawk's nest to feed her young.

CHAPTER SEVENTEEN

Josephine stood at the end of the picnic table, putting away the leftovers. A simple woman, Josephine minded her own business and acted as though she had difficulty understanding all the fuss. She told everyone she was happy Joe was dead, and that her daughter and grandchildren were free of his abuse.

Sandra helped her mother clean up as much as she could, but Josephine told her to sit down and rest.

Jason asked Sandra if she wanted to go for a ride in his VW, and she agreed. He took Sandra's hand and steadied her as she stood.

After helping her into the front seat, Jason drove out of the picnic area and down a dirt road into the park on the west side of the creek. He dropped the transmission into low gear, and negotiated the curve through the cottonwood grove that led into the river bottom. The cottonwood branches formed a canopy as beautiful as any cathedral. As they drove down the road, the sanctuary opened into another picnic area. The cottonwoods were shedding, covering the road with white seeds as pretty and feathery as any snowfall. Jason looked in his rear-view mirror. He could see the snowy blanket part in their wake. Then, just as though Jason and Sandra hadn't been there, the cottonwood seeds settled back on the road, covering their tracks.

Jason stopped on the concrete bridge that covered Big Creek. He rolled down the window, then turned toward Sandra and smiled. They could hear the sounds of the wind rushing through the trees. The whirling wind stirred the cottonwood seeds, pushing them up to the top of the trees before they fell like parachutes, to the ground in search of fertile soil. The sounds of the evening's insects rose to a fevered pitch as the birds called out in chorus, searching for their evening meal. Beneath the bridge, they could hear a gush of water cascading over a small waterfall.

"C'mon, let's get out and go for a walk. I'll show you where I whiled away summer afternoons fishing."

"Oh Jason, it's too hot."

"Come with me. I'll help. Besides it'll be fun."

"Oh, okay." She reluctantly climbed from the car and straightened her dress.

Captivated for a moment, Jason became aware of Sandra's beauty, despite her bruised face and broken arm. She wore a tight sleeveless tie-dyed cotton top. Her brightly colored pleated dress hugged her shapely hips. She arched her back as she stood up, accentuating her curves. His groin ached.

To diffuse his heightened tension, he looked away toward the creek. "Look, there's a carp sunning himself on the water's surface." He paused for a moment, looking up and down the creek bank. Then he shouted, "Look over there, it's my boat. It's gotta be."

"I don't see anything."

"There, over there under the cottonwood. Let's go have a look."

Jason ran down the dirt path beside of the bridge.

Sandra yelled after him, "Slow down, wait for me." She nearly slipped. Jason came back up the path. She grabbed his outreached hand, steadying herself as she climbed down the embankment to the creek.

Weeds covered the path, made so long ago by Jason and his friends. The carp splashed as though welcoming them. Crickets chirped. The stale smell of the creek filled their senses as they made their way to the boat.

Jason pulled the vines from the tattered rowboat. "It's rotted out. Not safe to go floating, but here it is."

Jason's attention seemed to flatter Sandra, but she seemed confused. More than anything, she felt confused about Friday night. She felt Jason was her friend, and somehow she trusted him.

They sat down on a fallen log beside the creek, and watched the carp sun himself. Sandra broke the silence. "Jason, why did you bring me here?"

"We need to talk."

"About Joe's death?"

"Yes. What do you remember about Friday night?"

"Not much. I remember Joe coming home. But after he hit me and twisted my arm, I don't remember much else. I did hear some a loud shot and remember finding him. I think I heard a car outside, but my mind's really foggy."

Jason took her hand and caressed it gently. "Sandra, have you talked with anyone else?"

"No, I don't think so. Your dad asked me a lot of questions, but I can't remember what I said. He gave me some morphine and I fell asleep. My sister and the sheriff asked me questions."

"What happened with the sheriff?"

"We drove out to my house yesterday morning. He showed me two bullet holes, one in the kitchen behind the door, and the other in the bedroom. He said that three shots had been fired from Joe's pistol."

"Three shots?"

"Yeah, that's what he said." Sandra looked at the carp in the creek. "He thinks someone struggled with Joe, and shot him. He told me that about the inquest tomorrow, after Joe's funeral, to decide how Joe died."

Jason put his arms around Sandra as she leaned her head on his shoulder. He looked deep into the creek, searching for something to say to comfort her.

Sandra began crying. "I'm afraid they think I killed Joe, and I'm afraid the sheriff will charge me with his death."

"No! Sandra, don't worry, that won't happen."

"How do you know?"

"Trust me, I'll find a way."

CHAPTER EIGHTEEN

"Mary, I need to talk with Robert some more about what happened Friday. Can I take you home, or would you like to stay longer at the picnic?"

"You fellows go on and talk. I'll get a ride home with Janice."

Charles caressed her hair, and kissed her gently on the lips. "Thanks for understanding. Don't forget the dance tonight."

"I won't."

Charles watched Mary walk back to the picnic, and made sure she had found her friend Janice, so she could get a ride home.

He found Robert, and they drove to Charles's favorite spot. Charles knew Robert to be a wise man, and Charles needed Robert's advice.

CHAPTER NINETEEN

"I didn't know you liked to come up here, also," said Robert as he and Charles walked toward the rock outcropping.

"Yeah, this is my favorite spot, a place of solitude. I often come to think about problems, and to seek solution."

"Me, too, though I haven't been up here for some time."

Making themselves comfortable, they sat quietly, gazing out over Smithville.

Charles broke the silence. "I've really felt welcome in Smithville these past five years, and I've tried my best to respond to people and their needs. When Mary and the children and I came here, we didn't know what to expect. Smithville's a small town and everyone knows everyone's business. That's a big change from Kansas City where no one seems to care what you do."

Robert replied, "Everyone's glad you came. We've been impressed with your medical care. You're always available, and everyone respects you. Sometimes, I wonder if you have time for yourself."

"I wish I had more time for myself. I love to read, but somehow just when I am reading a good book, someone calls and I have to respond. I have very little time to myself. But that's not what's on my mind, Robert."

"I sensed something else at the picnic. Tell me."

Charles cleared his throat, and rubbed his temples. "I've always tried to tell the truth. Nevertheless, sometimes things develop, where there isn't a right or a wrong. Sometimes, there are situations that have solutions that conflict with basic values, and you find yourself having to choose between two alternatives. Either choice on its own would be easy, but taken together, they raise significant conflict."

"I'm not sure what you're referring to."

Charles searched Robert's eyes thinking of a way to begin. "This is very hard. When I went to the Baldwin's on Friday night and I became convinced that Sandra had killed Joe."

"Really, Charles. From what I've heard, she certainly had a motive."

"Yes, she certainly did. But now I'm not sure she killed him."

Charles recounted the events of that early morning and his actions in changing the death scene. He told Robert that he had confessed to the sheriff. While he couldn't be certain, Charles felt the sheriff wasn't going to hold him responsible for what Charles did. After all, the sheriff had trusted him to do Joe's autopsy.

Charles put his face in his hands, and then looked up at Robert. "Even though I hope the sheriff won't punish me, I still feel guilty. Robert, I need help. I'm not a religious man. Maybe I need to look to God for forgiveness and understanding. I don't feel comfortable going to our minister, but you're an elder in your church. Can you help me?"

"God understands our imperfection, Charles. He understands your situation more than you think. I don't pretend to have all the answers, but I do believe that He was there with you, guiding your thoughts and concerns for Sandra. He doesn't condone killing in any form but He does understand and forgive."

Charles put his head in his hands and cried. Robert put his arms around Charles's shoulder, holding him for several moments. Charles wiped the tears from his eyes, smiled, and hugged Robert. "I do feel better, thank you."

"C'mon, let's drive into town and get a cup of coffee. Have you told Mary what you just told me?"

"Yeah, everything."

"Good."

Neither spoke as Robert took the wheel for the drive back into town. Charles sat quietly, watching the golden wheat roll with waves created by the ever-present southerly wind. He felt comforted by Robert's friendship. There one more thing he needed to learn from Robert. He waited for the right moment, continuing to look out the window.

Putting his hands behind his head, he leaned back in the seat. "Robert, there's a problem with this town that I don't understand. It seems to me that we all look the other way. After Joe's death, only a few people have come forward to express their support for Sandra."

"How long have you been here?"

"Five years this summer."

Robert pulled his car over to the side of the road, stopping under a large cottonwood tree. He turned toward Charles. "You're right, there are problems in this town, and I, for one, would like to see things change. Nobody talks much about it, but it's pervasive. What I know, I heard from my grandfather. I'm thirsty, let's get that cup of coffee, and I'll tell you what I know."

They drove into town and parked in front of the Kent Café. Although late, they could hear the occasional loud roar of a hopped-up Chevy with glass-pack mufflers.

Robert held the door for Charles, and they sat in a booth near the rear of the cafe. Robert ordered a cup of coffee. Robert turned to Charles. "You want a coffee, also?"

"No. What I really want is an ice cream float." Therefore, Charles ordered a black cow with two scoops of vanilla ice cream soaking in homemade root beer. Charles stuffed a spoon into the drink, then shoveled the ice cream into his mouth. "My, that's good. Haven't had one of these for a long time."

Robert stirred a sugar cube into his coffee. After blowing into the cup, he slurped a bit, and then reached for a second cube before starting his tale.

"During the Civil War, the Army established a fort at Hays. The fort protected the railroad and the Pony Express from the Indians. Occasionally, the soldiers would go west to fight in the Indian Wars, mainly in the Dakotas and Colorado. After the Little Bighorn, the fort continued, although on a smaller scale. The surrounding towns were nervous about the soldiers, who would often ride into towns and terrorize the local people. After the fort closed, some of the soldiers settled in Hays. But, one of the soldiers settled in Smithville after he left the military."

Robert pointed to his cup motioning for the waitress to give him a refill. "That soldier, his name was Zach, for Zachariah, staked a tree claim south of Smithville."

"Near Richard's farm?"

"Exactly. That's Richard and Josephine's farm. The farm didn't come from Richard's family. It belonged to Josephine's grandfather, Zach. Zach was a Buffalo soldier, and a Negro." Robert paused, as if for effect, before he continued. "Josephine's grandfather was a Negro."

Charles said, "I knew there was something different about Josephine, her speech reminds me of a Negro, but I didn't know."

Robert continued. "Zach's tree claim shocked Smithville, since most of the Negroes had settled in Nicodemus, an all-Negro town about thirty-five miles north of Ellis. Nicodemus remains essentially a nearly all-Negro to this day. Most of the people in Nicodemus farmed although many worked for the Kansas Pacific Railroad in Ellis. However, they remained to themselves. Kansans are proud of Nicodemus. I have often wondered if they aren't happy the Negroes remains segregated."

Charles said, "Did Zach keep to himself?"

"For a while he didn't do anything but work on the farm. Once Zach had the tree claim staked where he had to plant trees to lay claim to the land, he began coming to town. He attended the Methodist church. From what my grandfather said, Zach acted like a real gentleman although those in town never accepted him."

Robert smiled at the waitress. "Even though the town didn't accept Zach, one person did. Zach met and eventually married the daughter of one of the town's prominent white families. If you think the town was upset before, nothing prepared them for that marriage. Everyone went berserk."

"My God, I knew there religious prejudice existed here, but I didn't know about the racial prejudice."

"As a matter of fact, we have a lot of prejudice. Twenty years earlier, a son of a prominent family in Hays was murdered. Although lacking proof, everyone blamed two Negroes from the fort. Hays City vigilantes caught the two and hung them from the railroad trellis over Big Creek."

Robert sipped his coffee before continuing. "After the experience in Hays, and to keep it from happening here, the Smithville City Council passed an ordinance stating that the sun shouldn't set on a Negro face in Smithville. From what I understand, other towns passed similar sunset laws."

David Huffman

Charles rubbed his chin. "Let me see if I got this straight. Smithville resents Josephine's family because her grandfather was a Negro."

"And because her grandfather married a white woman, and not just any white woman. She was daughter of a prominent businessman."

"What happened after they passed the sunset laws?"

"The Smithville townspeople formed a vigilante group, just like the one in Hays, intending to scare Zach and run him out of town."

"What happened?"

"They rode out to the farm, where Josephine's grandmother, Stella, met them and ran them off with a shotgun. Before she could run them off, they wounded Catherine, Josephine's mother. After the incident, Zach and Stella kept to themselves and farmed the land. Old Zach died before his fortieth birthday. Stella continued to farm the land with the help of Catherine and her brother James."

"What happened to James?"

"He left to fight in World War I but never returned, so Catherine inherited the farm, and Josephine inherited the farm from her. When Richard came back from the second World War, he moved in with Josephine after they married. They took care of Josephine's mother until she died, some say of complications from the gunshot wounds. Sandra and her sister, Barbara, were born in the late forties.

Charles thought for a moment. "So all of this prejudice goes back to Zach? How can people be so shallow and insensitive to carry prejudice for so many years?"

"That's the nature of prejudice. It has no rhyme or reason, just exists, and no one has the courage to confront the wrong and change things."

"Well, I, for one, think it's about time to make some changes, whatever the outcome of this weekend. What's been going on is wrong."

Robert responded, "I agree. But how can we change a hundred years."

"One step at a time."

Charles straightened his tie. He told Robert about his trip to Richard's farm. He had found Richard to be a good man, only concerned for his daughter. He had an alibi for the time in question and, in Charles's opinion, didn't shoot Joe.

Robert paused, and then looked Charles in the eye. "I agree with you Charles. Richard, Josephine, and Sandra are good people. They need our help." He looked out the window at the passing cars. "It's not right. We have to stop this prejudice. It's not right for the sins of the fathers to persist with their children."

Charles responded, "I agree, but how are we going to reverse a hundred years?"

"I don't know, but we've got to try."

CHAPTER TWENTY

Jason brushed his hair out of his eyes and took a cigarette out of the roll in his T-shirt. "Goin' out with the guys. I'll be late, don't wait up."

His mother asked, "Why don't you stay home with your father and me? It's Sunday night."

"Can't, goin' to meet friends."

"Who?"

"Max, Alex. Maybe others. Don't know for sure. Got a keg of beer, and we're going down to the river and hang out on a sandbar. Jus' like old times."

"Why don't you stay here and spend some time with your father? You two should get to know each other better before you have to go."

"Dad's busy. Besides, I don't know. If he doesn't write me something and get me out of that damn draft-I don't know what I'll do."

"Don't threaten him, Jason. Things are sometimes out of his control. Maybe, even if he wanted to help, it wouldn't do any good."

Jason took a long drag on his cigarette and blew the smoke defiantly in his mom's direction. "We'll see. Right now, I don't think he cares enough to even try to help."

Mary removed her apron, and after carefully folding it, she laid the apron across the kitchen chair with a slow deliberate movement that belied her inner anger and frustration. "You don't understand your father. You are asking him to lie, and that's wrong."

Jason waved his arm in the air, as if to dismiss his mother. "I'm not asking him to lie, only to care about me enough to try to help me. The least he could do is talk with me. He avoids the subject like the plague. Sure, I want his help. Damn right, I don't want to go to that God-forsaken place. Most of all, I want him to care. Jesus, I doubt he cares about me." He paused, as if for effect, and then continued. "Shit, he never cared before, why should he care now?"

"I don't appreciate your profanity. Your father does care. I can't speak for him as a go-between. It's up to the two of you to work this out. I pray that you'll find a way."

"I don't know Mom. Right now, I gotta go. You got some money for gas?"

"I gave you money this morning. What did you spend that on?"

"Stuff. Just stuff at the picnic and besides, what business is it of yours?"

Mary bristled and took in a deep breath. "When you're in my house I expect you to treat your father and me with respect. I don't like your haughty attitude, Jason. Listen to yourself. Think before you speak. We love you, but we're not going to put up with this behavior."

Jason took a long drag from his cigarette and blew it out. However, this time, he blew the smoke away from his mother. "Sorry. I'll try to do better. I gotta go. I'll talk with you in the morning. Wake me up."

"Tomorrow is Joe Baldwin's funeral. Are you going?"

"Yeah, I guess."

"After the funeral, there's an inquest into the cause of his death. I'm afraid the sheriff thinks that Sandra killed Joe. Of greater concern to me, your dad is under suspicion for trying to cover up for Sandra. I'm worried about what might happen, not only to Sandra, but also to your dad. His reputation is at stake."

Jason looked at his mother. "Don't worry. Something will come up to help the sheriff know that Sandra didn't do it."

"What are you talking about?"

"Something. Gotta go. See you in the morning."

Jason sped down Main turned left on Fifth and headed toward Max's house. Even though he had seen Max last night, Jason felt uneasy about seeing his other friends. He found himself wanting to belong again, not only to his family, but to reconnect somehow with his friends. He had changed a lot, but had they changed? He figured they were stuck in the past.

Max looked up and waved from his front porch as Jason drove up the driveway. In some ways, they were they same. They both wore blue jeans, a T-shirt, and scuffed Converse high tops. However, that's where the similarity ended.

In Jason's opinion, Max epitomized everything that Jason had rebelled against. Jason had shoulder-length hair, while Max sported a crew cut. Max had his jeans rolled up at the cuff; Jason's bell-bottoms dragged in the dirt. Unlike Max, the knees of Jason's jeans were torn, and Jason had a peace symbol sewn on the right rear pocket. Jason figured that Max probably wanted to go to war, while Jason wanted nothing to do with the dastardly conflict.

Despite their differences, they greeted each other like friends, slapping each other on the back and raising their hands in a high-five gesture, like the greeting they exchanged daily when they were in high school. They had been the stars of the Smithville Cougars: Jason, the quarterback, and Max, the starting halfback.

After the high-five, Jason punched Max in his shoulder.

Jason said, "You scared the shit out of me last night with your stupid chicken game. I thought for sure you'd get yourself killed."

Max laughed as he slugged Jason's shoulder. Then he grabbed Jason's shoulders and held him at arm's length. "You look like shit. What the hell happened to you?"

Jason looked down at his clothes and rubbed his long hair. "I've changed, Max. We all change."

"Not if you stay in this podunk town."

"I thought you planned to leave after graduation."

"Yeah, I left, went to college. I'll be a junior next year. Can you believe that?"

Jason envied his friend. They had followed different paths. He wondered if he hadn't gotten so mad at his parents and had stayed, would he now look and act like Max.

Max pointed to Jason's VW. "What a piece of junk."

"Yeah, well, it gets me around. Let's get past this shit. I'm me, and you're you. I came over to have some fun, not argue about our lives. We are different, but for tonight, let's have fun."

Max said, "You better believe we're different. Why'd you come today? Trying' to get back in with the old gang?"

"I really don't know for sure. I had a good time last night. Part of me wants to get back into the mainstream of life."

"For starters, you could cut your hair and stop wearing those hippie clothes. You look so weird. How you dress makes a statement."

Jason said, "Not so fast. I gotta take it a step at a time."

"Okay, okay. Alex and some girls are waiting for us at the edge of town. You remember Judy, Sharon, and Mary Beth?"

"They still around?"

"Yeah, they went to school. Everyone's home for the summer. I thought they'd come last night, but guess they were busy. Didn't you see them at the picnic? They said they saw you, but you seemed more interested in Sandra."

"Yeah, well she's gone through a lot."

"I heard her old man got his head blown off. I heard that maybe she did it. She tells you that she did it?"

"No."

"No, she didn't kill Joe, or she didn't tell you."

"She can't remember much, and anyway, I don't think she killed him."

Max shrugged. "Whatever."

"Let's go." Since, after the race last night, Max had his Ford in the repair shop, they jumped in Jason's VW. Jason revved his engine as they sped out of the cul-de-sac and headed down Main and out of town.

They met Alex and the girls and headed south to the Smokey Hill River. When they had been in high school, they often went down to the river for sandbar parties. Max and Alex would bring beer and a wine drink called purple passion. Unlike Jason, who smoked marijuana, alcohol was their drug.

Jason looked up through the skylight in the roof of his van. The moon's light cast eerie shadows of farm silos as he sped along the blacktop. Jason watched the shadow of his VW dance between the long rows of wheat that grew tight against the road.

They reached the six-mile marker where Highway 386 headed east, they turned south onto a dirt road toward the river. Alex sped ahead, causing dust to jump from the road and obscuring Jason's vision. Jason thought about passing Alex, but Alex drove a Ford with a four-barreled carburetor. A car much too fast for Jason, so he pulled back from Alex so he could see the road better.

On the mattress in the back of the VW, Judy giggled as she and Max groped each other in a passionate embrace. Jason adjusted the rearview mirror and watched his friend.

Max pushed her aside, gasping for air. "Slow down, baby. At least wait until we get to the river and go skinny dipping."

"C'mon, honey! Don't let a girl cool off."

Max reached beneath her dress, fumbling with her petticoats. "Damn, can't find your legs inside all this."

"Be patient, I'll help."

Cooing, Sharon scooted closer to Jason in the front seat. "Want to pull over so we can have some fun, too?"

His groin ached, and as much as he wanted to have sex, his rubbers were in his backpack. He hesitated, and then thought for a moment. The last thing he wanted was to get this girl, or any girl, pregnant. "No, not now. Let's wait until we get to the river."

What had he said? What was happening? My God, I'm changing. Never before could he remember being so careful.

Usually, given the chance for sex, he didn't consider the consequences. He just went for it. Sharon had been the fantasy love of his life all through high school. Fearing rejection, he had never asked her out. Now that he had the chance to fulfill his fantasy, what does he do? Worry about getting her pregnant? He just shook his head.

She giggled, and put her head on his shoulder. Dust jumped from his VW as Jason floored the gas pedal and, like a dog in heat, he sped toward the river.

When he reached the cliffs south of the river, Jason hit the brakes. The paved road transitioned into a dirt one with deep ruts, making driving difficult. The path down to the river was so steep that he thought his VW might tip over. He put the gears into low and crept slowly down the path on the side of the cliff to the riverbank. When they reached the side of the river, Jason turned to Max. "And you thought this piece of junk couldn't make it."

Although called a river, the Smokey Hill was actually more like a creek. It drained into the Arkansas River and, consequently, didn't get the spring run-off from Colorado. However, during heavy rains, such as they had had during the past three days, the river ran deep, and Jason knew there could be sinkholes.

He cut the engine motor and waited for Alex.

The back tires of Alex's Ford spun in the sand. After several attempts, Alex was able get back on the small road and drive out onto a level area beside Jason's VW. Alex should have stopped there, but he didn't. He kept driving out onto the sandbar.

"Stop stupid." Jason yelled as loud as he could, but Alex kept driving. In no time, the car was in over its bumpers. If Alex didn't gun it, or worse, if he hit one of those sinkholes, they were goners. Jason jumped out of his VW and ran headlong into the water after his friend's car. Alex gunned the engine, causing his tires to spin and spray sand out the back, like machine gun bullets, nearly blinding Jason. Jason found the back bumper, and somehow managing to get a foothold, he pushed the Ford ahead onto the bar.

Out of breath, Jason yelled, "Christ, I thought you knew it wasn't safe here, particularly after the heavy rains."

Alex replied, "Didn't know. Thought this old car could go anywhere."

"You sure tested its limits."

"Thanks for your help. You okay?"

Jason pulled his shirt up and wiped his face, then smiled. "Yeah, I'm okay. Glad you didn't sink and drown."

"Me, too."

They helped the girls across a narrow way on the sandbar before returning to the VW to get the beer and blankets. Jason tuned a transistor radio to an AM station from Hays. They lit a fire with driftwood, and poured beers all around. They listened to the radio, while they lay on their backs, gazing at the stars.

Max broke the silence. "Ever think you could see a satellite?" He pointed into the western sky. "Is that one?"

"Hell, I don't know," replied Alex. "It's moving too fast. Looks like a plane to me."

Someone said, "Who cares?" Everyone laughed.

They drank beer, and smoked cigarettes. Soon, the others moved away from the fire and spread blankets; they began making out. Turning to Sharon, Jason said, "C'mon, let's take our blanket and walk to the end of the sandbar."

After Sharon spread their blanket out on the sand, she sat down beside Jason. "Tell me, big boy, what's been going on in your life? What happened when you left, and why'd you come home now? Man, if I'd had the courage to leave, I'd never come back."

Jason thought for a moment, and then, told her about his life in Arkansas, about the commune and the woman he thought he'd spend the rest of his life. "Just when I thought everything was okay, my girlfriend went crazy, like on weird drugs or something. She started hitting and yelling at me and I had to get out of there."

Sharon cuddled up to Jason. "Sounds like a real downer. I'm glad you decided to come home."

"So am I, I guess." Jason lay back on the blanket, putting his hands behind his head, searching the sky for something to say.

Finally, he broke his silence. "Tell me what's been goin' on with you?"

Sharon thought for a moment, then cleared her throat. "I went to college in Hays for a year. I liked it, but school is hard. I got on the cheerleader team and liked going to games. I missed the fun we used to have. Funny, I don't remember you coming along much, though. You were always off on some cloud, thinking about things the rest of us didn't understand. You're real bright Jason; did you ever think about going to college?"

"Nah." Jason wasn't truthful. His rebellious attitude and behavior had gotten in the way, and he had lost track of his abilities. In addition to being a good athlete, he got good grades in high school. He had been on the honor roll, and had even taken an examination for the National Merit Scholarships. Christ, he didn't even know how he had done. He wondered if his folks knew.

Jason and Sharon returned to the fire, drank beer, and sang songs to the radio. Max and Judy went skinny-dipping. Jason couldn't help sneaking a peak. He could make out their bodies sliding around in the river, and every once in a while, Judy would stand up and rub her breasts, coaxing Max. She teased him and giggled, but a better swimmer, she kept away from him.

Sharon put her arm around Jason. "C'mon, let's get wet." She stood, peeled her shorts and top, and jumped the water so quickly, Jason barely had time to react.

He fumbled with his zipper, finally managed to get naked, and followed her into the water. She knelt in the water about four feet from the edge of the bar in one of the sinkholes, so the water covered everything below her shoulders. As he got closer, he could make out the top of her shoulders in the bright moonlight. She reached out for Jason and pulled him to her. They embraced and kissed. He felt her rigid nipples against his chest. So excited, he could hardly catch his breath. He tried to gain a foothold in the sand, but the sand gave way beneath him, making staying in one place difficult. Sharon threw her head back and laughed.

After several tries to have sex, Jason became frustrated. Despite his long-standing fantasy, he realized he wouldn't get laid. He finally got his balance, but the sexual tension was gone. Out of frustration, he picked Sharon up, kissed her lips, and carried her back onto the sandbar. They sat for a moment, shivering in the evening breeze; then, putting on their clothes, they walked back into the light of the fire.

Sharon stared into the fire, making Jason feel uncomfortable. He thought she would make fun of him for not being able to perform. He hated criticism, and thought he would need to retaliate.

Sharon turned to him. "Jason, I'm sorry, but I gotta say something, and it's not about the sex."

Here she goes, thought Jason.

Sharon continued. "I don't know, but, I think something is really wrong with you. In my opinion, you've gotta get your stuff together, and quit messing around with your life. Something's eaten at you, until you figure it out, you're going to ruin your life and never amount to anything, and if that happens, I, for one, will be sad.

CHAPTER TWENTY-ONE

"Morning, Jason."

"Morning, Dad."

Charles thought about quizzing his son about his activities last night. Mary had told him about their confrontation before Jason left. As Charles struggled with how to approach the subject, Jason's outfit distracted him. Jason looked like a train wreck. Jason's clothes were shabby. His tie-dyed multicolored shirt, torn in the back, and his bell-bottom jeans with frayed ends that barely covered his scuffed sandals, weren't the clothes to wear to a funeral. Charles gritted his teeth. "You're not going to wear that, are you?"

"Back off. I don't have a suit. I do have a pair of pants and a clean white shirt, though. And I'll wear them if I can borrow a tie?"

Charles relaxed, realizing that Jason planned to change clothes before the funeral. "Bow or four-in-hand?"

"I like the way you look, think I'll try a bow tie."

Mary threw some more bacon in the pan and continued frying eggs for Charles. "Sleep well?"

Both Jason and Charles said yes in unison. After eating, they cleared the table. Charles grabbed a towel and put it around his waist, saying to Jason, "I'll h, you dry."

Mary said, "Good, then I'll have time to get ready for the funeral and we can all drive to the church together."

The dishes finished, Charles invited Jason into the library. "Today is difficult. I hope there won't be a scene like yesterday at the park. We need to bury Joe in peace and get past today."

St. Paul's Catholic Church, a tall building with two steeples on each side of a large entrance, had marble steps that rose between the two pillars to the entrance. The bright sun beat down and the wind blew so hard that the ladies could hardly keep their hats from flying away.

Charles climbed the steps, and opened the door. By contrast, with the outside, the dark church had a musty smell created by the dampness of the rains. Charles stood still for a moment allowing his eyes to accommodate to the darkness before looking around the church. Being a Methodist, he had rarely been in this church. Statues, brought by religiously persecuted immigrants, who had fled from Europe at the turn of the century, decorated the church. At the front, a large statue of Mary, with her outstretched arms, stood to the left of the altar. Votive candles, representing the faithful and their prayers, lined the sides of the sanctuary. Wooden pews, on both sides of the center aisle, held the mourners.

Joe's casket, draped with flowers, dominated the front of the church in front of the altar. Lit candles guarded the ends of his casket.

Charles took Mary's arm and escorted her toward the front of the church. Many of the people, though not all, were kneeling.

Charles sat back while Mary moved forward to kneel. Charles looked at her in disbelief. Although not a Catholic, out of apparent respect, Mary knelt for several minutes. Then, briefly saying a prayer, she settled back beside him.

After the ushers seated Sandra and her family, they helped Joe's parents to their seats near the front of the church. Charles hadn't thought much about them and their loss. He wondered how much they knew about Joe, his drinking, and his abuse of Sandra and the children.

The organ began its slow processional. Two altar boys led the processional with Father Flanagan walking behind and lifting an open Bible above his head. As they walked down the aisle, Charles couldn't help admiring the stained-glass windows and the gold-plated statues on either side of the sanctuary.

The church was similar to European churches. The parishioners were descendants of immigrants who had fled persecution in Germany and Russia. They brought with them not only their religion but also the hearty red winter wheat that the local farmers grew. That wheat could withstand the hard winters of western Kansas and brought life to the plains.

There were several towns around Smithville. Munjor, Liebenthal, and Antonio all had similar churches. Charles took medical care of the people from these little towns. He regretted that he hadn't taken the time to learn more about them.

The parish's faithful were a simple people, hard working, and innocent. He knew how much they loved their church. He resolved to get to know them better, not just as patients, but also as fellow citizens in this community.

Sandra wore a black scarf over her bowed head. Richard sat beside her, staring at the coffin, with a stern look on his face. Barbara sat on the other side, her arm draped around Sandra. Charles wondered if any of them had killed Joe.

He looked around at the rest of the congregation. Others had a motive. Robert, the Co-op manager, and Reed Johnson had lost money in one of Joe's real estate schemes. Bob, Joe's drinking buddy, although dead had reasons to shoot Joe. But how would they ever find out?

Charles sat quietly through the hour-long service. At first, he occupied time by thumbing through the missal. Fidgeting, he straightened his tie. Straining to listen to the service, he had difficulty understanding why the Catholic Church continued to use Latin.

Charles hadn't been religious. In the past, he had considered himself an agnostic, but in deference to Mary, he rarely discussed spiritual matters.

If what Robert had said about God's forgiveness was true, however, and Charles had received absolution for his behavior, Charles needed to rethink his attitude about religion.

As he thought about Sandra and Joe, Charles thought about the priest's lack of response to Sandra's call for help from the church. If Father Flanagan could have avoided this tragedy, if he had had been more responsive to her needs and authorized her to leave her marriage. On the other hand, thought Charles, everyone had responsibility in this matter. Everyone, including himself, had failed in some way. In all fairness, he couldn't blame the church for his shortcomings.

Charles hoped the priest would say the homily quickly and not cast blame on anyone. He hoped Father Flanagan wouldn't carry on too long for the sake of Joe's parents and Sandra. The priest talked about Joe as though he were a tree that appeared normal on the outside but had decayed inside. Just as a tree that had become rotten in side, Joe's soul, weakened by the decay, could no longer stand.

Charles, reflecting on the findings of Joe's autopsy, became amazed at the insight the priest appeared to have.

Father Flanagan ended by praying for Joe's soul. He prayed that Joe would pass quickly through purgatory, and if it were God's will, that Joe would find a place in heaven.

Everyone stood respectfully as the pallbearers pushed the coffin out the church and into the hearse. The Catholic's buried a few of their faithful in a small church cemetery on the grounds of the church. There were only a few remaining plots, however, and those were reserved for the religious, and people who were entitled to special consideration. They buried the common folks in the cemetery. Catholics buried their in one part of the cemetery, near several statues of Jesus and his disciples, while the Protestants buried their dead to the east of the center road that separated the two areas. The same stone fence surrounded the area, and gnarled cedar trees grew everywhere. Smithville had religious segregation that continued even to the grave.

Charles felt uncomfortable in this place. In his opinion, when someone died, Charles felt he had failed. This place, in his opinion, contained his failures.

CHAPTER TWENTY-TWO

After the burial, everyone returned to the church for a meal prepared by the churchwomen. After paying their respects, Charles drove Mary and Jason home before heading back to his office to see if anyone needed attention. He usually didn't see patients on Monday afternoon, but he had gone to the funeral that morning, and he became concerned that someone might be sick and need his help. Often, people showed up and waited on the porch, hoping to see him.

He also wanted to see if Paul from the university had left a message with Gertrude about the specimens. More than anything, he needed some time to think before the inquest tomorrow morning. He thought about Joe and Bob and couldn't help wondering what the bartender at the Brass Rail knew about them.

He dropped by the office; the lights were off and no one stood on his front porch. He didn't even stop; instead, Charles kept on Main until he reached Second Street, then he turned south and pulled into the parking lot behind the Brass Rail. He wanted to find out more about what happened Friday night, before Joe died.

He didn't recognize any cars in the Rail's parking lot. Apprehensive about going into the bar, he looked in the rear-view mirror as he buttoned his suit coat and straightened his bow tie.

Although he had driven past the Brass Rail, he had been in the bar once before when Dave called him to help Bob. Calm yourself, he thought. No one in here can hurt you and information is all you want.

He hesitated, then opened the back door of the building. He looked around the smoky bar. The lights were dim. A laugh, then a giggle, came from the back table, where a man sat with his arm around a girl. The man kissed her on the neck, while she half-hearted pushed him away. Charles strained, but couldn't make out whom they were. He approached the bar cautiously.

Dave, the bartender, looked up from washing glasses, "Howdy, Doc, want a beer?"

"No. Thanks anyway." Charles looked around nervously, then turned to the bartender. "Not many here tonight?"

"Don't remember seeing you in here before."

"You called me to help Bob. He had passed out. You remember?"

"Yeah, Doc, I guess I do. What brings you here at this time? Most of my patrons come later in the evening. We only serve 3.2 beers. If you want something stronger, ya have go to the club in the bank building. They've got mixed drinks."

Charles straightened his back. "I came to talk about Joe and Bob."

"What 'bout them?"

"They were in here drinking last Friday night. I'm told Richard came in and had some words with them."

Dave thought for a moment. "Yeah he came in that night. Mad as hell, too. Shook his fist at them."

Charles looked again at the back table. But the couple had gone. "What can you tell me about Joe and Bob?"

"What ya mean?"

"I heard they gambled and had debt: some say that Joe owed Bob; others say Bob owed Joe. I just wanted to see if you knew anything."

Dave held a glass up to the light and after polishing the glass he put it back on the rack above the bar sink. He gazed at Charles out of the corner of his eye. "Don't want to get dragged into anything, but if I can help, I'll tell you what I know. But you gotta promise me that what I say is off the record."

After pausing for a moment, he continued. "Yeah, they gambled, though not here. I don't have any gambling. Both of them had markers out with people in Salina and maybe even as far away as Kansas City. I don't know for sure, but they were talking about their problems when Richard came in. After he left, they continued to drink. I kicked them out around midnight because they were drunk. They left screaming at the top of their lungs."

"What were they yelling about?"

Dave thought for a moment. "Can't say for sure, something about never paying up on their debts."

"Which one didn't pay his debts?"

"Don't know."

Charles reflected. "Sure wish I knew who was made at whom."

"So do I."

Charles wheeled around to see the sheriff standing behind him. "I-I didn't hear you come in."

"Saw your Jeep in the parking lot. Since you don't frequent this place, I thought something might be wrong."

"Everything's okay. I just wanted to talk with Dave here about Joe and Bob."

"Learn anything?"

"Not much. Just that they did gamble and Joe owed Bob and several other people money."

"That's interesting. Heard the same story. Doc, there are some things I want to go over with you about last Friday night. Got a minute, Charles?"

Dave backed away. "This is none of my business, and I'll leave you two alone."

"Not so quick," the Sheriff replied, "I'm also interested in Joe and Bob's relationship. I won't make it difficult for you, Dave, but I need to know. Did Bob have a reason to kill Joe?"

Dave didn't know. He knew they fought a lot. He told the sheriff about Bob and Joe and their gambling. Dave said he knew that Joe owed Bob some money, but he didn't know how much.

"Last Friday they were in here drinking heavily and left staggering out the door," Dave said. "That's all I know, and ya gotta believe me, Sheriff."

Realizing that he could learn no more from Dave, the sheriff turned and nodded for Charles to follow him to the parking lot. He motioned for Charles to sit in the front seat of his patrol car.

The sheriff began. "I want to go over the bedroom scene again. I've decided not to tell the judge you changed things; but in return, I need you to help me by telling me everything you remember about the bedroom when you found Joe. I need to know all the details you can remember. Do you remember where the gun?"

Charles thought for a moment. His gaze focused on the light pole at the entrance to the parking lot. Looking beyond toward the western sky, he could see a thunderstorm developing southwest of town. Lightning popped. Four or five seconds later, a loud clap of thunder rolled through the town.

Charles cleared his throat, then turned to face the sheriff. "I don't remember for sure, but I think I remember the pistol at the foot of the bed."

"On the right side or the left side."

"On the right, I guess. That's why I assumed that Joe was right-handed."

"We both agree that with his wounds and him being left handed, Joe couldn't have shot himself. But for the life of me, I can't figure out who shot him. Do you know?"

"No."

"Do you think Sandra did it?"

Charles paused. He wanted, if possible, to convince the sheriff that Sandra didn't kill Joe. "I don't know for sure, but I don't think she shot him. She doesn't remember what happened. She was in a daze when I fixed her arm and sewed up her cuts. I'm not even sure about yesterday at the picnic. In my opinion, even if she did shoot Joe, it wasn't premeditated."

"That's for me to decide, Doc." Rubbing his chin, he looked at Charles. "Tell me again what you found in Joe's brain."

"I have to wait for Paul to call me in the morning, but I think Joe had a brain cancer. Maybe that's why he was so mean to Sandra. I don't know."

"Well, you'll have to tell all this to the judge in the morning.

"Did you go to Joe's funeral?"

"Wouldn't have missed it for all the tea in China. I spent my time watching all the people in the crowd, trying to see who shed tears and who seemed happy Joe's gone."

Charles said, "I suspect the whole town is happy he's gone, though I'm going to miss having a pharmacist in this town. I hope Sandra can find a way to keep it going. I'd hate to have to send my patients to Hays for their drugs.

The sheriff, distracted in thought, didn't seem to hear Charles's reference to Sandra and the pharmacy. He straightened his back. "There are two more things I don't understand."

"What's that?"

"Did you see a note on Joe's typewriter at his house that night?"

"No."

"Someone, and not Joe, wrote a letter to make it look like Joe committed suicide."

"I didn't see a typewriter. Where was it?"

"In the bedroom, on a desk near Joe's closet."

Charles scratched his head, trying to remember. "Yeah, I remember that old typewriter. Come to think of it, I don't remember seeing any paper in it."

"So, that means someone wrote the note after we took the body out, cause I don't remember seeing it either. I found a note Saturday morning while checking the house over, before I went back there with Sandra and her sister. That's when I found out there were three shots; one in the kitchen, a second in the bedroom, and the third fired at Joe."

Charles perked up. "If there were three shots fired Friday night in that house, Joe and someone were fighting. I wonder if someone else was there. For the life of me, I can't figure out who might have been there. The logical suspects all have an alibi as far as I know. So that leaves someone we don't know anything about."

The sheriff coughed and nodded in apparent acknowledgment of Charles's deductions.

Charles continued. "What about Barbara? Could she have written that letter? Sandra had a broken arm." Charles paused, then raised his hand, as if to make a point. "Wait a minute. Barbara picked Sandra up early Saturday morning at the office after I set Sandra's fractures. On my way home, I drove by Sandra's house. She and Barbara were packing some things."

The sheriff stood, abruptly ending the conversation abruptly. "Well, Doc, I guess that's all for now. We have the coroner's inquest tomorrow morning. The judge will hear the evidence and decide if there's any crime. Both of us will have to testify."

He cinched his gun belt a notch tighter, and then patted his gun, sending a chill up and down Charles's spine.

The sheriff continued. "I don't think it'll serve any purpose to tell the judge about your actions, other than finding Joe and helping Sandra. I'm late with my paperwork, haven't filled out an official report. I'm headin' back to the office to do that. Call me if you hear anything from the university."

Sheets of rain fell as Charles jumped out of the sheriff's patrol car. He dodged puddles as he ran toward his Jeep. Weary from the events of the week, Charles waved goodbye to the sheriff. Then, he drove onto Main Street toward home and, hopefully, a peaceful night.

CHAPTER TWENTY-THREE

Jason sat on the front porch with his feet propped up on the railing, smoking a cigarette.

"Howdy, Dad."

"How you doin' Jason?" Although acting glad to see his son, Charles hoped he could get right to bed. Tired from his ordeal, he needed a good night's sleep before facing the coroner's inquest in the morning. "You talk with anybody?"

Jason replied, "Ya, I did. Sandra and I went for a walk down by the river after everyone else left the picnic."

Charles acted as if he hadn't seen Jason and Sandra leave after the picnic. He wanted to learn more about Sandra's state of mind. "She upset?"

"A little. We talked about Joe and her life. I asked her about the night Joe died, if she remembered anything."

Charles knew he'd not get to sleep soon, because he also wanted to hear what Jason had learned. "Did she remember anything?"

Jason took a long drag from his cigarette, coughed a little, and then related his conversation with Sandra. "The way she remembers, after Joe hit her, he went into the bedroom. She heard noise and arguing. Ordinarily, she said Joe would yell and scream when drunk. She wondered if someone else was in the bedroom with Joe, but she can't remember much. Her memory is really a fog. Anyway, she thought the yelling got louder, and then she remembered hearing the deafening sound of the gun blast."

"Did she go into the bedroom?"

"She couldn't remember much else. Anyway, that's when she said she called you."

"She said that while on the phone, she heard a vehicle start up and drive off. What do you make of it?"

Charles gazed across the front yard, as if in a trance. "Bob had a green Ford truck; did she say it looked like his truck? I wonder if Bob shot Joe after all." Charles reflected on his experience with Bob at his office on Saturday morning. "I don't know. Bob didn't act like a person who had just killed someone."

Jason said, "Could Joe have killed himself?"

"No, the autopsy evidence pretty much excludes that possibility."

Jason cleared his throat. "I don't think Sandra killed him, though by God she sure had reason enough. Dad, you've had a rough weekend. I'll fix you a scotch, and take the phone off the hook. You relax. I'll put on that Vivaldi album."

"Thanks."

Jason found Charles's favorite record and put it on the hi-fi. Charles sat mesmerized, listening to the Philadelphia Symphony playing Vivaldi's "Four Seasons." When it ended, he climbed the stairs, and collapsed into bed with Mary.

"Honey, wake up. The phone."

"What time is it?"

Mary lifted her head to look at the bedside clock. "Three fifteen."

"My God. I can't deal with this. Tomorrow's the inquest and someone's calling."

"Better answer it. Maybe it's an emergency."

Charles groped for the phone and cleared his throat. "Doc here."

He listened for a moment, then chewed on his lip. "You mean you want me to come over to give your daughter a penicillin shot and some cough medicine?"

A long pause and Charles became more alert. "Terry, it's nearly four o'clock. Can't it wait till the morning?"

Mary touched Charles on the shoulder. "Who is it, dear?"

"Terry, the plumber. Says his kid has a cough and it's keeping him awake, and he wants me to come fix his child."

Charles sat on the side of the bed then cleared his throat. "Okay, okay." Charles stood up beside the bed, thinking of a way out of this. When he realized he couldn't say no, he smiled and said, "Tell you what, the sink in my bathroom leaks and the dripping is keeping me awake. We'll make it even. You come fix my faucet, and I'll come fix your kid. Agreed?"

At five in the morning, Charles and Terry were the only people awake in Smithville, passing each other, as they went to fix the other's respective frustrations.

CHAPTER TWENTY-FOUR

Tuesday morning, in contrast with the past four days, the sun shown brightly.

Charles stood on his front porch, admiring the yellow streaks of sunlight shooting across the blue sky, like rays of hope. Today, he hoped, truth would replace deception, and, like the bright sun, the town would have a fresh start, somehow cleansing the sins of their fathers.

Charles took a sip of freshly brewed coffee and set the cup down on the table. The newspaper boy waved from his bicycle before throwing the morning Smithville Tribune toward the porch.

Charles waved back. He ambled down the steps and picked up the paper. Even though he felt invigorated and hopeful, he had some apprehension as he opened the paper to read about the events of the past three days.

The headlines carried the usual bad news of Vietnam. The TET offensive had begun in Vietnam, and the body count in Southeast Asia continued to rise. Avoiding his feelings about the war and Jason's request for a letter to the draft board, Charles didn't read the article; instead, he opened the paper to the local section.

Charles read an article about Joe's death and an interview with the sheriff highlighting the facts. The sheriff had been careful to limit any speculation, saying only that there would be an inquest on Tuesday to determine the cause of death and decide if any wrongdoing had occurred.

Charles thought about his own actions. He felt he had been wrong to move the gun and make it appear that Joe had committed suicide. His heart had been in the right place, trying to protect Sandra. Whatever the outcome, he felt that his intentions had been right.

Charles decided he would accept whatever happened in the courtroom. Even though the sheriff had promised that he wouldn't bring any charges against him, Charles still worried.

Nonetheless, he felt at peace. Charles had only one thing to resolve today. On Wednesday, Jason would for his draft physical. Charles had to decide how he would respond to

Jason's request for a letter to the Army that might change Jason's eligibility for the draft.

******

Jason awoke to the sound of the paper hitting the driveway. He stood and looked out the window, watching his father stoop to pick up the paper. He admired the morning sun's rays and the beauty of the blue sky. He had a lot on his mind. He reflected about his coming home and whether he could find his way emotionally back into his family and this town. He mulled over his conversations with Sandra. He thought about his experience Sunday night on the sandbar with Sharon and her comment to him after they had been skinny-dipping. He considered the funeral and Sandra and Joe and their tumultuous lives together, and he resolved that he wouldn't ever treat a woman that way. He thought about his draft notice, and wondered if his father would help him.

******

Sandra also admired the morning sun, but she worried about today. Although her memories of Friday night's events were fuzzy, whatever the outcome, her abuse, and the abuse of her children had ended.

As she entered the kitchen, she found Barbara cooking breakfast. She could hear her daughters and their cousins laughing and playing in the living room. They had already eaten their breakfasts, so Sandra and Barbara enjoyed peace and quiet as they drank their morning coffee and ate eggs and bacon.

"Have a seat; I've made your favorite omelet." She looked Sandra over. "Your face looks better; does your arm still hurt?"

"Yeah, it hurts some, but I'm getting used to it."

"Good. Chow down. You need strength"

Sandra picked at her food, but after the first taste of her omelet, she quickened her pace, as though she hadn't had anything to eat for a long time. "Barb, what do you think will happen today?"

"I trust the truth will come out about Joe and how he beat you and your kids."

"I'm worried about what the sheriff and judge will do. Do they think I killed Joe?"

Barbara said, "I anticipate that they will think that Joe killed himself."

"I sure hope they don't think I did it. I thank God that he won't beat me anymore. I wish I could remember about more what happened that night. He hit me on the head, and I've been in a fog ever since."

"You do remember the picnic on Sunday?"

"Do I! I'm embarrassed by the way I acted, but I'm not embarrassed about what I said."

"You put on quite a scene, but you said what we all felt. Do you remember what Doc said about us all having some responsibility in this matter?"

"Yes, but I don't know what I could have done differently."

"It doesn't matter now. We can talk about it later. When you get before the judge, you just tell him what you remember. Make sure he understands how Joe beat you and how he made your life miserable. Maybe the judge will think that Joe deserved what happened to him, regardless of who killed him."

******

Richard and Josephine were up at the crack of dawn. They had chores to do before coming to town for the inquest.

Richard milked his cows and fed the chickens.

Josephine wrung the necks of two chickens, and dressed them for frying for a dinner they would have at Barbara's after the inquest. She dusted the chicken parts with flour, then put them in her iron skillet on the woodstove. She knew which part of the stove had the right amount of heat to fry the chicken, as well as where she could place the pans to bake fresh bread.

She took a rag from the shelf, and after wrapping it around her hand, she carefully removed a flat iron and pressed her only dress, the one she usually wore to church. She wanted to look as presentable as possible for the benefit of her daughter.

She yelled out the screen door, "Richard, ya gotta get ready, or we'll be late."

Richard stomped his feet at the front door, then climbed the stairs to their bedroom, and wanting to look presentable, changed into his Sunday suit. He didn't know what to expect at the hearing, but whatever happened, he too was happy to see an end to his daughter's abuse.

Charles had told him there would be a town meeting after the inquest to talk about the town's attitude toward Sandra and her family. He wondered if the meeting would have anything to do with Josephine and her great-grandfather, Zach, and the town's prejudice against their family. He hoped so. Having fought in the Great War, he feared no one. He realized that if his family and his granddaughters were going to have peace in this town, something had to change.

CHAPTER TWENTY-FIVE

Since Smithville didn't have a courthouse, the sheriff decided to hold the inquest in his office in the Town Hall. The cool morning had given way to the sun's heat that paralleled the rising anxiety of those present outside the sheriff's office.

The sheriff's office occupied the first floor of a large building with the same limestone façade that bedecked the rest of Smithville. Charles sat quietly with Sandra and her family on a bench outside the sheriff's office. They watched apprehensively as Judge Johnson drove up and parked his car on the other side of the street. He turned the rear-view mirror toward him, scowling as he turned his head from side to side. He ran his fingers through his graying hair; then, after moistening his lips with his tongue, he twisted the sides of his handlebar mustache. Getting out of his car, he stretched, put on his black robe, and grabbed his briefcase from the back seat. He looked both distinguished and intimidating as he walked briskly toward the sheriff's office.

Charles observed that the judge's cheeks were plethoric, and his nose ruddy and prominent. He wondered if the judge drank alcohol. If so, that would certainly complicate the hearing, Joe's alcoholism would surely come up at the hearing.

With a quiet that belied their internal stress, they watched the judge approach the building. Judge Johnson nodded to everyone and managed a smile, which seemed plastic to Charles.

After what seemed like a long time, the sheriff opened the door and invited Charles into his office. Charles looked around the room. He had been there before, but, somehow, the room seemed different this time. In the center of the room, a large partner's desk stood surrounded by several wooden chairs. There were few comfort amenities. Behind the desk were two empty cells for holding prisoners. Charles wondered how long they would stay empty.

The sheriff began. "Sit in the chair, Doc. The three of us need to talk before calling any witnesses. I've explained the background of this case to the judge. I'm sure he will want to hear your take on Joe's death."

The sheriff then told Judge Johnson about the town, and Charles, and the closeness of the community. He explained that Charles had been there five years, and before that, there were no medical services for the community. He told the judge how much they all appreciated Charles.

Charles spoke quickly but confidently. He emphasized that he had very little forensic experience. The judge waved his hand, as if to dismiss the concern. Charles then proceeded to describe the night Sandra called him, and how he found Joe dead of a gunshot wound.

Judge Johnson asked, "How'd he die?"

Charles looked nervously at the sheriff.

The sheriff cleared his throat. "Go ahead, Charles, tell the judge everything, including the autopsy you did Sunday morning."

"Joe died of a gunshot wound in the right side of his head." Charles lifted his right hand and pointed his index finger beneath his right eye. "The bullet entered his skull below the right eye, and exited in his left parietal skull area, just behind his ear."

"Do you think Joe killed himself, or did someone else kill him?"

Charles hesitated, trying with all his power to remain focused. "He couldn't have killed himself, your honor. Joe was left-handed. His wounds aren't consistent with Joe inflicting the wound on him, in my opinion."

The judge coughed so hard that his face turned red and then pale. For a moment, Charles thought he might stop breathing and require resuscitation. Soon, the judge's face pinked up, and Charles relaxed back into his chair.

The judge took a long sip of water. "Let me get this straight. You both think someone else shot him, that he didn't commit suicide?"

Both the sheriff and Charles chimed in at the same time. "Yes, your honor."

The judge looked at the sheriff in the eye. "Do you have any idea who could have shot him?"

"Well, there were several people who could have, but we flat-out don't know."

"Who do you suspect?"

The sheriff looked at Charles. Charles started to answer, but the sheriff put up his hand and answered the judge's question. "My first thought would be Sandra. She could have shot him in the face while he slept. As you'll see from questioning her, she had a motive. Joe was an alcoholic and a wife-beater. But I'll let her tell you her story."

"Who else?"

Charles spoke up. "Just the whole town."

"What do you mean?"

"Joe had a lot of enemies in this town. The first and most obvious was Bob. They gambled a lot and had some shady deals together. Furthermore, they had a fight that night and Joe owed Bob money."

The judge looked at his list of people who were to testify. "I don't see a Bob on my list."

"That's because he's dead. He came into my office on Saturday morning, complaining of his abdomen hurting, and before I could determine anything, he vomited blood, and died."

"That's a shame, would've liked to talk with him. Do you think Bob met with foul play?" The judge paused. "Seems strange to me that two individuals who apparently knew one another and were drinking buddies would die within twelve hours of one another." He looked at the sheriff. "Don't you think it's strange?"

The sheriff replied, "I guess it does. Didn't think much of the coincidence. What do you think, Doc?"

Charles cleared his throat. "I took care of Bob. He came to the office and vomited blood. I'm sure he bled from an ulcer or something in his stomach. He drank a lot and certainly had every reason to have an ulcer. I looked him over. Didn't find anything to suggest foul play."

The judge rubbed his abdomen. "Oh, okay. Who else had a reason to kill Joe?"

"Richard, Sandra's father." The sheriff chimed in. "But he's got an alibi. In my opinion, he had a reason to shoot Joe, his daughter being abused and all."

"Anyone else?"

The sheriff continued. "Barbara could have done it to protect her sister. I think she wrote a note on Joe's typewriter to make it look like Joe had committed suicide."

"Who's this Barbara?" the judge asked.

"She's Sandra's sister. She'll be here, also."

"One final thing before we let people in. If everyone knew about this abuse of Sandra, why didn't someone do something about it?"

Charles responded, "Everyone looked the other way, thinking that we shouldn't get involved with other people's business. We all wish we'd acted differently. Don't we, Sheriff?"

The sheriff looked up and nodded in agreement.

Charles continued. "Once this hearing is over, we intend to have a town meeting to see if we can put a stop to something that has been going on far too long in this town."

The judge stopped writing notes on his yellow pad. "What's that?"

"Prejudice. Prejudice against Sandra and her family for being born into a family of Negro descent."

"I realize that's a problem in all of Kansas, and, for that matter, in my opinion, the whole country. I attended a meeting in Topeka to discuss the Brown versus the Board of Education ruling. In my opinion, Kansas has an opportunity to lead the nation in righting the wrong against Negroes. However, that's not why we are here. Let's get on with it."

The sheriff asked, "What order do you want people to come in?"

The judge straightened his robe, looked in a mirror, and then turned to the sheriff. "Actually, before we have them come in, I need to know a few more facts. Tell me some detail about the house. Where did you find the gun, and there anyone else there that night?"

The sheriff told the judge about the kitchen, the two bullet holes, and the gun with Joe's prints on the handle and the trigger. The sheriff paused for a moment. "There is a second set of prints on the gun barrel."

"Whose prints are those?"

The sheriff said, "I don't have a match."

"You mean to tell me that there's someone else's prints are on the gun?"

"Yeah."

"Did you check Sandra's prints?"

The sheriff said, "Yes I did, and her prints aren't on the gun."

"You mean to tell me that she didn't have any prints on the gun?"

"Yes, Joe's prints are on the handle. There is a second set of prints on the barrel of the gun. That Joe's prints are on the gun don't mean much, in my opinion. He could have fired the gun anytime and left his prints there. On the other hand, he may have been holding the gun when it fired."

"Did you check for powder marks on Joe's hands?"

"Yes I did, and he had powder marks, but that doesn't mean much, only that he had fired the gun in the last six hours."

The judge rubbed his chin. "Well, if Sandra's prints aren't on the gun, that lets her off the hook, doesn't it."

"I guess so."

"Does she know this?"

"No."

The judge said, "Good. If she's a bit worried about her guilt, it might make for interesting testimony. Let's be sure we don't tell her before we hear her testimony." He looked menacingly at the sheriff and Charles. "You haven't told her about the prints, have you?"

Both the sheriff and Charles responded in unison, "No, we haven't."

"Good. Does anyone else have a motive to have shot Joe?"

Charles said, "Yes, the whole town. I just plain don't know."

The judge reflected on the matter. "What do you mean the whole town? Does that include you two?"

Both the sheriff and Charles responded with a resounding no.

"I guess if we knew whose those prints were, we'd know a lot more than we do about what happened that night," the judge reflected.

The sheriff responded, "You betcha."

The judge thought for a moment, then said to the sheriff, "Did you check Bob?"

"No. I didn't get the prints off the gun before Bob was in the ground."

Charles thought about Saturday morning. He remembered noticing a dark smudge on Bob's right hand. Should he tell them about the smudge? What good would it do? Reed had washed the body. The smudge could have been grease, since Bob worked a lot on his car. Charles realized he would never know. He decided to see how things developed. If nothing came out of the testimony, he would bring that up as a possible explanation.

The judge said, "I see, well it seems to me that if we can find that person, our job will be a lot easier. If we don't have an answer by the end of this hearing, I may have to order Bob dug up. We could get his prints and see if there's any other evidence. However, I would sure like to avoid that, if I can. Digging someone up is always complicated."

"I agree," the sheriff responded.

Charles noticed the sheriff didn't tell the judge about Charles's actions. Charles reasoned, the sheriff had, apparently, become convinced that Charles's actions, however misguided, didn't influence the facts of the case, and would only confuse the judge in his deliberations. With that, Charles felt more relaxed.

The judge took notes as he listened to the sheriff. "The fact that Joe's prints are on the handle of the gun intrigues me. Anyway, let's not get carried away. We'll deal with that question after I talk with the wife and other members of her family. Anyone else I should be talking with anyone else. If so, bring them in. But I must remind you I have to be back home by one-o'clock this afternoon."

"We should be able to finish well before that," the sheriff responded.

The judge thanked Charles for his information and asked him to stay and hear the remaining testimony.

Charles said, "There's one thing more, Judge. When I did the autopsy, I found an area in Joe's brain that looked like he had a cancer. I've sent samples off to the university, and I hope to hear this morning from my friend who is a pathologist. I don't know what bearing that has on things, but I'll let you know as soon as I find out the results."

The judge reflected on Charles's testimony. "If he did have a cancer, that could explain some of his behavior, even his drinking, but it doesn't really have material effect on our deliberations. It may make it more difficult for Sandra. Does she know about this?"

Charles shook his head. "I haven't told anyone. At least not until I hear from Kansas City about the results of the tissue examination."

After finishing Charles's testimony, the judge asked for a cup of coffee, and made some notes on his yellow legal pad. He then looked up and asked the sheriff, "Who's first?"

"Sandra." The sheriff opened the door and invited her in. Her face still bruised and her arm in the cast, she limped into the office. They did their best to make her comfortable.

******

Sandra began her story.

Joe had been out drinking with Bob. Worried about the girls, I had them stay over at Barbara's house. I had just got home when I heard a loud noise on the side porch. I saw Joe stumbling up the front steps and heard him bang on the door. He was real drunk. I slowly pulled back the curtain, and then turned on the front porch light. After opening the door, I stood back, avoiding the rain and Joe.

I asked, "Where have you been?"

He replied. "What ya think? I've been at the Brass Rail with Bob."

He yelled at me, called me a bitch, and for me to get out of his way. He took a swipe at me with his fist, hitting me, causing blood to gush from my mouth.

Joe kept swearing, wiped his shoes on the carpet, and threw his coat on the floor. He sat at the table, waiting for me to feed him.

I remember looking out the window, but it was raining cats and dogs, and I couldn't make out anything.

"You got some food, bitch?" he screamed.

I cried, pleaded with him to be quiet. He took another swing at me and told me to shut up. Then he yelled, "Think I give a rat's ass what you want? I'm hungry."

He grabbed and twisted my arm. I screamed and fell to the floor. He reached down to grab me again, but I pulled away. Gathering all my remaining strength, I screamed, "You bastard, that's it. I've had it with you. Get outta here."

He taunted me, "Yeah sure, you don't have the guts to leave, and I'm sure not going to leave, so just put up with it."

I started cooking, and he grabbed me and hit me with something hard on the side of the head. She pointed with her good arm at the bruise above her left eye. I started bleeding. After that, I must've blacked out. The next thing I heard a loud bang. I went into the bedroom and found Joe, lying across the bed with blood covering his head, gasping for breath. I started toward him, I but hesitated.

Sandra broke down and cried. Charles gave her a handkerchief and comforted her before she continued.

I thought, if I don't do anything, he'd die. I sat down in the chair beside the bed with my hand over my mouth. He gasped for air and then let out a high-pitched groan and stopped breathing. I realized that my struggle was over.

David Huffman

I limped back into the kitchen, and called Doc and asked him to come over.

******

The judge asked several questions about the details of the house and the evening. The sheriff asked her questions about the location of the gun, but she couldn't remember that detail. He asked about the position of Joe's body on the bed, but she couldn't remember. Finally, realizing her she couldn't recall every detail, they decided to end her testimony. The judge told Sandra that he realized it had been difficult for her to tell her story and he appreciated her doing so.

"Is it okay if I help her out to her car?" Charles asked.

"Sure, I need a break anyway," the judge replied.

Charles escorted her past her father and sister and into her car.

"How'd I do?" she asked softly.

"Just fine, just fine. I'll call you later and tell you what the judge decides."

She thanked him.

"Sandra, later after this is over, I think we should have a town meeting. Can you come?"

"What for?"

"We need to talk and have some reconciliation about this whole affair. I think the sooner the better."

Charles returned to the room, and the three discussed Sandra's testimony.

The judge started. "I'm not sure what to expect. That whole story about her watching him die could have been a figment of her imagination, born from wanting her abuse to end. Anyway, without her fingerprints on the gun, it's hard to think she had anything to do with Joe's death."

The sheriff and Charles agreed and they decided to move on to the next witness.

Richard testified next. He said had argued with Joe and Bob at the Brass Rail, but after that, he left town and drove home to his farm, arriving there about eleven. Josephine would verify what he said. In addition, he'd called his neighbor to check on the river. It had been raining hard, and he thought it might flood. He gave his neighbor's name for verification.

Since Charles had established the time of death as much later, the judge said that they would check things out, and thanked Richard for his testimony.

Barbara took the stand, but she didn't offer any new insight. She said that Sandra called her and asked her to come to the house and get the girls. The next day, she came over to the house and packed some clothes.

After a pause, the sheriff confronted Barbara. "Did you write the suicide note?" She twisted her dress with her hand and then she broke down and confessed. "I didn't mean any harm. I just tried to protect my sister." She didn't know if Sandra had killed Joe. She recounted the beating that Joe had given her sister.

The judge said, "I know Sandra had been beaten and abused. There seems little question. But that's not why we're here, is it?"

Barbara straightened her dress. "No, I guess not. Please believe me; I don't think Sandy killed him. She just couldn't do it. Joe was real mean." She paused to collect herself. "And I'm glad she don't have to suffer anymore."

After excusing Barbara, the judge turned to the sheriff. "What do you think?" The judge quietly stroked his mustache. He stared at the sheriff and asked, "Despite your theory that Joe didn't kill himself, I wonder. Maybe that's the easiest way to deal with this. I don't know. From what you've said, the evidence points that Joe held the gun and pulled the trigger. The unknown is those damn prints on the barrel of the pistol. Nonetheless, in the absence of their identification, I just might rule that Joe killed himself."

The judge took a break to get relief in the bathroom down the hall. After returning, he began to summarize his findings. "There are so many unknowns in this case. Joe Baldwin may have killed himself. On the other hand, his wounds don't support a suicide.

Several people had reason to end Joe's life. If we had more evidence, I'd even grant you that Joe had a reason to end his life, if you can believe the story about his gambling debts. Sandra had reason to stop her abuse.

I can understand that. The law doesn't recognize an abused woman's striking back at her abuser as a defense. However, that doesn't matter, since her prints aren't on the gun. If we accept the evidence, it's clear that she didn't shoot her husband, though, by God, she had a reason in my opinion."

Charles said, "Maybe the law should be changed to recognize spousal abuse as a reason for self-defense."

"Maybe someday, but not now."

The judge thought further. "Apparently, Bob had reason to kill Joe. They were others involved in gambling, and Joe owed Bob money. I wonder if anyone else in the gambled with Joe and had Joe's IOU. Apparently, others in this town had a motive to see Joe dead. The people that wanted to protect Sandra did not have the opportunity, or they have good alibis. The bottom line is this. There is not sufficient reason to bring anyone to trial in this case. For lack of a better explanation, I think it's possible that Bob may have shot him or perhaps Joe shot himself, though I don't' know. In any case, we may never know. I'm going to enter say the record that the Joe died of a gunshot wound to the head and we can't determine the responsible party. I see no reason to have any further legal actions."

As they were about to wrap up the inquest and complete their work, the door opened. Jason stood, framed by the doorway.

"Who are you and what are you doing here?" the judge asked.

"I have some things to say that will shed light on Friday night and explain what happened at Sandra's house."

Charles stammered, "Jason! What are you doing here? What do you have to do with this?"

"Sit down, Doc," the sheriff interjected. "Let him speak. Maybe he has something to add to this."

The judge coughed and straightened his tie. "By all means, go ahead, son." The judge looked him over, frowning at his clothes. "Tell us what you know."

******

David Huffman

Jason looked at his father, and began his story.

Before I came home Friday night, Dad, I stopped by Sandra's house. We had been friends before I left Smithville. I knew Joe beat Sandra and her kids. Part of my reason for leaving Smithville had to do with Sandra. I couldn't stand the fact that the town didn't do anything to stop her abuse.

Sandra wrote me often during those two years. She had called me five days ago, crying, and hard to understand. She begged me to come and help her. So, I came, not really understanding how I could help, but knowing I had to try and help her.

Last Friday, after I got to town, I pulled my VW bus up to the Baldwin's curb, and rolled down the window. As I sat there, I remembered that night three years ago when I had been baby-sitting their kids, and witnessed Joe's abuse. I had stopped Joe then. We got into a fight and I hit him, and knocked him out. I knew what to do three years ago. Somehow, I had to protect her again.

I climbed out of the VW and walked slowly up the front walk. A gust of wind blew my hair. In the lightning of the growing storm, I could make out Sandra sitting on the front porch swing.

Pathetically, she looked up at me with her black-and-blue eyes. Damn, I thought, he's hit her again.

I asked, "Is he inside?"

She shook her head slowly back and forth.

"Where is he?"

"Out drinkin' with Bob. They'll be back soon."

"Let me look at that eye."

I carefully pulled her hair back and examined the bruised forehead and eye. "Joe hit you?"

She slowly nodded.

"Damn it Sandra, this has to stop. Let me take you to my dad's house."

She shook her head and, standing, walked into the house. I followed her. "Where are the kids?"

"At Sis's"

"Let me clean you up at least."

I filled the sink with warm water. I anxiously looked out the window as I rinsed a rag and wrung it out. I wiped the blood from her cheek and checked the cut on her forehead. "It'll need stitches. Let me call my dad, Sandra, for God's sake."

She stood and pushed me away. "Nobody can help me, not your dad, not you. Thanks for coming, but it's too late."

"What do you mean it's too late?"

Her eyes opened widely.

I wheeled around.

Joe stood menacingly blocking the door. He yelled, "What the hell you doin' here? Messin' around with my woman?"

"Take it easy, Joe. Sandra called and asked me to come. Said she was in trouble."

"Goddamn right she's in trouble, more trouble than she bargained for."

He reached behind the door, grabbed his pistol, and aimed it at Sandra, then back at me. "You're gonna pay for this, you bitch."

Joe waved the gun around the room. Then he pointed the gun back at Sandra. "You first."

Joe pointed the gun at Sandra, then at me. I could see his finger tighten around the trigger. As he began squeezing the trigger, the phone rang. Distracted, Joe took his gaze off us and stared at the phone.

I sprang toward Joe, grabbed the barrel of his gun, and pushed it to the side. Startled, he pulled the trigger, making a deafening blast. The shot went to the right of my ear, hitting the wall behind the door.

I managed to keep my grip, and pushed the barrel first toward the ceiling then toward Joe. We struggled. Joe was bigger than I was, but his being drunk, gave me the upper hand.

We struggled out of the kitchen, down the hall, and into the bedroom. I held the barrel, but Joe's finger gripped the trigger. Joe lost his balance and fell onto the bed.

I pushed the barrel toward Joe's face, and a second blast more deafening than the first went off beside my head, missing me. I knew if I didn't end this, Joe would kill me so I pushed the barrel into Joe's face. For a moment, he stared at me, then he pulled the trigger blowing a hole in the right side of his face.

He collapsed, and let go of the gun.

David Huffman

The gun's heat burned my hand and I dropped it. Breathing heavily, I stood over Joe expecting him to regain consciousness and swing his fist.

The smell of gunpowder sickened me. I swallowed hard to push back the vomit.

I stood and looked at Joe. His face ripped by the gunshot. His bulging eyes stared at me. I backed out of the bedroom, keeping my eyes on Joe.

Deaf from the gunshot, I yelled, "Sandra, you okay?"

Sandra was crouching in the corner of the kitchen crying. She looked at me, and then kept sobbed loudly.

"Is he dead?"

"I-I think so."

I held Sandra, wiping blood and tears from her face. "Jesus, I just killed Joe."

"He had it comin'."

"Should we call the police?"

Sandra said, "No, they'll never understand. They'll think I did it."

"But you didn't do anything, Sandra. Let me call the sheriff."

"No," she said, sobbing, "I'll call your dad. He'll know what to do."

Jason looked at the shocked faces of the three men. "So I left and Sandra called you and you came."

******

Charles gave the judge a pleading look, then nervously returned his gaze to his son. "I don't know what to say, son."

Jason brushed his hair back and continued, "I fought with him to protect Sandra and myself. I thought he'd kill us both."

The judge straightened his back and looked at Jason. "I'm a bit perplexed. Why did you come forward and tell your story? You didn't have to. No one except Sandra knew you were even there."

Jason said, "I guess I felt responsible for taking a man's life, even though I did it in self-defense. I didn't want anyone to think Sandra shot him, although, by God, she had plenty of reasons. Lastly, I didn't want my dad to be under any suspicion. I guess I just wanted to tell the truth. It'll take me a long time to get over this."

The judge said, "We realize that, son. We need to check your prints, and if yours are those on the barrel, I will accept your testimony."

They excused Jason and sat in silence.

Charles said, "This is all a big shock to me. I had no clue about Jason."

The sheriff and the judge looked at each other. The judge said, "We realize that, Doc. How could you?"

The sheriff thought for a moment. "If what Jason says is true, how do we reconcile that Sandra didn't remember, or at least say, that Jason had been there. You have any thoughts, Doc?"

Charles responded, "My only thought is that Sandra has trouble remembering anything about that night. Joe hit her hard on her head, and I think she is amnesic for the whole evening. I don't know but I don't think she purposefully lied, I just think she is confused. With her head wound, it is hard for her to remember everything, so like people with amnesia, she fabricates."

The sheriff straightened his string bow tie. "Well, Jason's testimony sure explains a lot." He turned to the judge. "Seems to me, this boy shot Joe in self-defense."

The judge said, "You'll have to get the boy's prints, and if they're the ones you couldn't identify on the barrel of the gun, I'll have to agree with you."

The judge stood, straightening his robe. "Gotta get back to Hays. Sheriff, you finish things up, and assuming there's no other business, I'll be on my way. Send me the papers so I can sign off on this. I suspect everyone will be happy to hear how this turned out. You tell them. I need to get on my way."

The sheriff thought for a moment. "One thing about this testimony has me baffled. Either Sandra's got amnesia like you say, or she's a damn good liar because Sandra's story and Jason's rendition don't jive." He paused, rubbing his chin. "You know what I think?"

Charles struggled to remain focused. "What's that?"

"I think it's possible that Sandra remembered everything. I think she acted like she couldn't remember in order to protect Jason."

The judge said, "That's ironic, isn't it? Jason protected Sandra. I changed things to protect Sandra, and she protected Jason."

The sheriff said, "I don't know, I just don't know for sure. I guess we may never know for sure. I guess it doesn't make much difference, does it?"

The judge replied, "No, I guess it doesn't."

The developments shocked Charles. His first impulse on Friday night had been to think that Sandra had killed Joe and to keep her from suffering anymore, he had changed things in the bedroom to protect her. After that, he had tried to find out who killed Joe. He even thought that Joe might have killed himself, until he did the autopsy, that is. Then, he thought Bob had been involved in some way. But, in his wildest dreams, he never thought Jason might be involved.

Charles said, "Sheriff, I need some time to digest this."

The sheriff replied, "So do I."

They stood and thanked the judge. After the judge left the room, they sat quietly, each absorbed in thought, trying to understand and come to grips with what had just happened.

The sheriff finally broke the silence. "We need to do something to heal this town."

Charles replied, "I agree. I have an idea. Let's have a town meeting at the bowling alley. Can you come?"

"You betcha."

Charles called Mary and told her about Jason and that they'd be home soon. He needed a piece of her carrot cake and a tall gin and tonic.

CHAPTER TWENTY-SIX

Charles felt Sandra and her family had suffered enough. Through no fault of their own, they were the victims. The town's people had kept the prejudice alive. Like a vulture with spread wings, the hatred hovered over Smithville. Charles felt the town had condoned the abuse of Sandra as payment for her great-grandfather's race.

Although Charles didn't actively participate in the narrow-mindedness, somehow, he had become an indirect instrument of the town's bigotry by not stopping the abuse of Sandra by Joe. With Sandra's physical abuse over, Charles knew that he had to try to end Smithville's discrimination against her and her family.

They needed a meeting place, and there weren't many possibilities. Smithville had no civic auditorium. The VFW hall was a possibility, but Charles had problems having the gathering there, particularly since he was contemplating helping Jason avoid the draft. Another venue could be high school auditorium, but the school wasn't an option because the janitor was painting the auditorium.

That left the bowling alley attached to the Brass Rail. After the coroner's inquest, Charles stopped by to talk with Dave to get his permission to get together at the bowling alley. A bowling league was in progress, but most of the people involved with that would also come to the town congregation. After listening to Charles, Dave agreed to provide his place for the meeting. He would cover the bowling lanes with wood boards, and there would be enough room for everyone in town to attend the assembly.

Before the town gathering, Charles called an assembly of the town leaders of Smithville. He didn't know how many of the townspeople would come. If the leaders of Smithville could reach a consensus, Charles felt more confident that the townsfolk would follow their recommendation.

In Charles's opinion, Smithville was at a crossroad. In many ways, the issue with Sandra and her family had become like a boil on the skin of the community. If he didn't lance it and allow it to heal, it could become an ugly scar. If it didn't heal, the festering boil could also grow inside and seed the lifeblood of the community with its deadly germ, and the community might die.

Charles needed to prepare the community to insure his plan worked. First, he called Robert, and together they called the community leaders to solicit their support. They called the mayor and the ministers of the Protestant churches, as well as Father Flanagan. Robert represented the school, and Charles, the medical community. Robert called several businessmen, including Reed, the mortician, and Ralph, the manager of the Co-op. They thought about calling Richard, but decided not to invite members of Sandra's family. After all, they were the objects of the prejudice: ending it wasn't their problem.

They met in the café next to Joe's drug store. Charles asked Carol, the café's waitress, if she would close so that they could hold a meeting. More than happy to lighten her load, she agreed, and they moved tables and chairs, so everyone would face each other. Carol made a fresh pot of coffee, and cut several pieces of a fresh apple pie.

The mayor arrived first. Despite a hot afternoon, he had on a three-piece suit. A Phi Beta Kappa key dangled from a chain in the watch pocket of the vest. He had been the mayor for as long as Charles could remember, and although the mayor was always outspoken, Charles thought many of his comments were disingenuous, causing Charles to wonder if the mayor had really earned the academic key, or if he had bought it in a pawnshop.

The Methodist minister, Douglas Jacobson, a highly respected member of the community, arrived next. He rarely came to the café for coffee and seemed offended that they would have the town meeting at the bowling alley. After all, it was next to the Brass Rail, the seat of the devil.

Charles marveled at the segregation that took place as the Protestant ministers sat together, well away from Father Flanagan. The priest had just left afternoon vespers. He wore his usual black suit with a black shirt and a white collar. An old man with gray hair and wrinkled skin, ruddy face, and his nose even redder than before. Charles made a mental note to talk with him about his drinking. At least, when the priest drank, he became quiet and went to sleep. Strange, Charles thought, how some people, like Joe, became violent with alcohol, while others seemed to become more passive.

"Anyone want some more coffee before I close up?"

"No thanks, Carol." Charles hoped this would go smooth. He knew there weren't too many times they got together under the same roof.

The mayor patted his abdomen. "I'd like some more coffee before you go. Also, get me another piece of that great apple pie. Nothing that pleases a politician more that a good piece of apple pie."

Doug looked up from his coffee. "Cut it out, you don't need to campaign here. Your job isn't in jeopardy, no one else wants it."

The mayor stirred his coffee. He reached in his vest pocket and pulled out his watch. Opening it, he frowned. "Let's get on with it, got to get home before long, the Mrs., you know."

Charles cleared his throat. "I wanted to get together with you before we had the town meeting. There are some things that need to be said to inform the town about the coroner's inquest and some things I want to talk about."

Charles told them about the hearing and the judge's decision. He told them that his son had defended Sandra, and that, unlike the rest of the town, Jason had taken on the responsibility of putting an end to Sandra's abuse.

Charles cleared his throat and continued. He recounted the story Robert had told him about Sandra's family and her great-grandfather. Then he paused.

Charles looked the group over and asked, "Does anyone know whether there is any prejudice against Sandra and her family because of her great-grandfather?"

Silence. Several spoke denying any knowledge of prejudice. But the air seemed to thicken over the room while everyone looking at the floor or at the ceiling but not at each other.

Doug broke the silence. "When I came to this church over thirty years ago, everyone said to avoid that family. They said that one of our families had a daughter who married

Zach, Sandra's great-grandfather, when he left Fort Hays and set up his tree claim south of Smithville."

Charles looked around the room. Everyone continued looking at their feet or out the window. Each person kept their hands around their coffee cups as though they needed security.

Doug stirred his coffee. He blew into the cup to cool the coffee, then took a long swallow. He coughed and cleared his throat. "My, that's strong coffee."

The mayor reached over and handed him the sugar bowl. "Couple of spoonfuls will help."

"Thanks, it's hard for me to talk about this, but I think the reason our church shunned them because they were Negro."

You could hear a pin drop. Everyone knew this had happened, but for Doug, and by his word, the Methodist Church, to admit it, was an overwhelming revelation.

He continued. "Although we didn't want to admit it, we were afraid that if we welcomed them, more of the Negroes would come to Smithville. That old codger's prejudice still lives and in the church. While alive, he never missed an opportunity to voice his hatred for Zach and his shunned daughter. So we catered to him then and shunned Zach, and continue to shun his descendants, particularly his great-granddaughter."

Charles asked, "What did Zach and his wife do for a church after that?"

"They joined the Catholic Church."

Everyone shifted in his chair. Doug stirred his coffee. Everyone in the room remained silent and uncomfortable.

Father Flanagan broke the silence. "Stands to reason. After all, we are more tolerant. They probably felt more welcome."

Doug chimed in. "You can't get off that easy. Besides, I don't know how you can use the word tolerant. You didn't help Sandra when she came to you asking for help with Joe and his abuse."

Father Flanagan frowned, staring at Doug. "How do you know that?"

"I have my sources."

Charles interrupted. "C'mon. We have to get past this. Maybe the fact that Zach and his wife left the Methodist Church for the

Catholic Church has led to some of the prejudice between Catholics and Protestants."

Someone said, "Maybe you're right, Charles."

Robert looked at Charles. "If we are going to be a community that cares for one another, we have to stop this bickering. After all, we're all God's children, black and white, Protestant and Catholic."

Doug thought for a moment. "You're right." He turned to Father Flanagan. "I think that's at least part of the reason that we haven't been able to get along over these years. When she joined your church and you accepted her, we were unable to understand that and thought our religion had been shamed. I, for one, resented that."

After a lengthy discussion, they promised they would do their best to end this prejudice and create a more cohesive and accepting community.

This reconciliation hearted Charles, though he wondered how long it would last. At least, they had a good start. He looked at his wristwatch. "It's nearly two. Everyone is gathering at the bowling alley. You can all see how stupid this is. We're all able to understand things. I'm not sure the town can, however. I'm worried that the sparks are going to fly when we get together. How are you guys going to help me— help us—get through this and put an end to the prejudice that's plagued this town?"

Charles watched the group leave the café. He turned to Robert. "I wish I could just reach in my bag and grab a scalpel, and cut this cancer from our town."

"You've started but we have a lot of work to do before this is resolved."

"I agree. Let's get going."

Everyone came to the town meeting in the bowling alley. Heavy smoke filled the inside, making it difficult to see. Eyes watering, Charles greeted everyone he could with a friendly handshake or a pat on the back. Richard and his wife were sitting near the front, but Sandra wasn't with them. She has to be here, he thought. If this meeting is to be successful, Sandra has to be with us.

Charles went outside and paced nervously up and down the sidewalk. Just as he was about to give up and go back inside, he saw Barbara's car turn onto Second from Main.

Sandra sat in the front seat. Breaking into a smile, he relaxed. After helping them out of the car, he escorted the women into the bowling alley.

Charles stood before the gathering. "Thank you all for coming. The judge won't prosecute anyone for Joe's death. My son, Jason, defended Sandra, and shot Joe in self defense."

A murmur went through the crowd.

"Quiet please." Charles continued. "I asked you all to come here to talk about where we go from here. You all know that I do my best to heal your bodies. Now I want to help heal this town. I am very sad by the events of the past week. It's no secret that Joe was an alcoholic and that he beat Sandra." He looked at Sandra, who had her head down. "I especially regret not coming to your aide earlier, Sandra."

The gathered nodded, some coughed. Others cried. From the back, a lady yelled, "That's right, Sandra, we're all sorry."

Sandra stood. "Thank you. It's been a long and difficult week. I've had time to think about things, about my role. In many ways, I let this happen to me." She looked tenderly at Charles. "I don't blame you for what happened. Oh, I got mad at the picnic, and for that, I'm sorry." She looked at the floor, then took a deep breath. "I've thought about leaving Smithville and starting new somewhere, where the memories aren't so difficult. But this is my home, and you are my friends."

Everyone broke into applause.

Sandra continued. "I'll do my best to keep the pharmacy open. I hope to hear from the school at the university about a possible replacement pharmacist to keep the place open until I can decide what to do. More than anything, I feel free, and I intend to stay here with my children and family and my friends."

Sandra sat down beside her dad. He grabbed her squeezing so hard she let out a yell.

Everyone cheered.

Charles stood. "Out of adversity comes wisdom and growth. I want all of us to do a better job taking care of each other. If we do this, we will be a better community, one we can all take pride in." Charles wiped a tear from his cheek.

A loud a-men emanating from the back of the hall, fractured the silence. Robert stood, putting his hands together as if in prayer, then he started clapping. Others followed, and Charles felt the rafters of the building resonate with the community's resolve to come together.

CHAPTER TWENTY-SEVEN

Charles looked at the clock on the wall at the end of the bowling alley. Three o'clock. He took in a deep breath and let it out slowly. "Well, I guess that about does it." He looked anxiously about the room, expecting to see some of the more zealous don white hoods, but no one made any moves. "Anyone have anything else to say?"

The room echoed with a few coughs, but for the most part, silence prevailed.

Robert broke the silence. "We've all got a lot of work to do. This has been a difficult meeting, and as uncomfortable as it has been, everyone has had a chance to air their feelings. I think we'll all feel better with this out in the open. I'm sure Richard and his family agrees. I, for one, am glad we have made a start. I think there's a chance that things will be better for all of us. Time will tell."

Charles stood, smiled at Mary and Jason, then turned and acknowledged Sandra and her family. "I think we all need to get home.

It's been a long day. I would like to spend some time with my family."

Charles opened the door, and after placing a doorstop to keep the door open, he stood at the exit, shaking everyone's hand as the town's people left. Most were quiet as they left the hall. A few said they were proud of the town and wanted things to be better for all Smithville's residents. Charles agreed, saying, "We'll have some more meetings. It's taken a long time to get to this point; we can't expect to overcome a century of prejudice in one day."

Richard and his family were the last to leave the hall. Charles watched him take Sandra's arm and guide her to Barbara's car. After helping her into the car, Richard walked back to his truck. He opened the door for Josephine and steadied her as she stood on the running board. As she struggled to get into the truck, Richard put his hand on her bottom and gave her a gentle push.

Josephine turned and scowled at Richard. "I'm not that weak so as to require ya hand." Then she broke into a smile. "But, I like your hand where ya have it. I thought you forgot where to put it."

"No, Mama, haven't forgot. Just that it's been a tough time. I'll show you I haven't forgotten when I get home." Walking around the front of the truck to get into the driver's side, Richard noticed Charles standing beside his Jeep.

Richard stuck his hand out for a handshake. "Thanks for your help, Doc." He kicked the dirt, then stared into Charles's eyes. "I don't know what to expect, but I'm concerned that things will go back to the way they were. As for me, I'd just as soon do my farming. For my girls, I'm concerned that they will be shunned should people forget today."

Charles nodded his head. "I know what you mean. For my part, I'll do whatever I can to make sure things don't go back to the way they were."

"Thanks, Doc, I appreciate that."

Charles looked Richard in the eye. "Before you go, there's something I need to talk with you about."

"What's that?"

Charles hesitated. He needed to get Richard's opinion about his troubling dilemma. "I need to talk with you about your feelings about the war."

"What war?"

"Vietnam."

"Oh, that war." He scratched his head. "Thought you were referrin' to the Great War."

"No, I want to talk with you about Vietnam. Jason wants me to write a letter, trying to get him out of going to Vietnam."

Richard raised his arm and flexed his biceps in an intimidating manner. "When I first heard about Vietnam, I wanted to go. I got out my uniform and dusted off my medals." He pointed to his intimidating Semper Fi on his right arm. "Even thought about updating this tattoo."

"So, you think Vietnam is okay, and we should be over there?"

"I don't know. War is hell. Our kids fight wars at the whims of old men. Sometimes, I think those old farts who call themselves generals don't realize how damn difficult it is to fight a war. You know what I think, I think they ought to send us old codgers into war and let the youth be. The youth are our future, for Christ's sake. Why send them to certain death?"

Richard put his hand on the door's handle, as if to get into the truck and leave, but, instead, he sat down on the running board of his truck.

Josephine yelled at him, "Ya commin', or not?"

"Keep your pants on, Ma. Gotta talk a minute with Doc." He thought for a moment, then continued. "I don't know what we're trying to get from this war. The Cong haven't invaded us, or threatened us, for that matter. I guess we're there to keep South Vietnam from going Red, but I wonder how they really know for sure that them Commies are going to take over the world. For one thing, I don't know how in hell fighting a war in that jungle will prevent that. It seems so far away."

Somehow, Charles hadn't expected this response. He had assumed that Richard, being a Marine, would be gung-ho and strong in his support for fighting over there. Nevertheless, he knew that Richard was sharing his innermost feelings, and Charles felt an intimacy with him. Wanting to get closer to his new friend, he sat down on the running board. "What was it like when you were in the war?"

Richard's eyes glistened as though he looking off into space. "Haven't talked much about war. For sure, haven't talked with Josephine and the girls. For me, fighting the Japs was hell."

He stood and pounded his fist on the hood of his old Ford truck. "At least we had it easy in one respect. We knew who the enemy was. The Japs had uniforms, guns, ships, and planes, and we could recognize them. It's different in Vietnam. You can't tell who the enemy is. The Cong comes out of the forest and trees, like varmints, and shoots ya. Then, before you can get a bead on him, he climbs back into his hole, and ya can't find him. Christ, even women and kids are shooting at our boys over there. Can you figure that?

"No, Richard, I can't."

Richard sat quietly, as if reflecting on his honesty with Charles. "I don't have a son, Doc, but if I did, I wouldn't want him to go to war."

Charles let out a deep sigh. "Nor do I."

Richard reached into his back pocket and pulled out a can of Skoll. He put a pinch in his mouth, then chewed it vigorously before stuffing the wad in his cheek. "What did you do, Doc? Were you in the war?"

"No, I was in medical school, and the draft board gave me a deferment. I tried to enlist, but they wanted me to finish med school. Said I would be more valuable if I didn't go right away. Then, the war ended."

"Good for you, didn't miss much."

Charles nodded as if in agreement. "But I always felt guilty about not going. I respect you guys that went, and I think every day about those who gave their lives and time so I could continue my studies and become a doctor. It's a debt that I have been trying to repay ever since."

"I wouldn't worry about that."

"That's easy for you to say. You paid your debt to society by fighting in a righteous war. What have I got to show for my time?"

"For Christ sake, you're a doc. You take care of us and keep us well. All I provide is wheat and beef."

Charles said, "I think farming is important. You give us the very essence of life. I think what you contribute is far greater than anything I do."

"I'm proud that I fought in that damn war to make it possible for you to live and do what you do. Hell, because of that we have peace and can live here without someone telling us how to live."

Charles thought about what Richard said. He realized that Richard had fought hard and risked his life for his country and for freedom for his family. The town, including him in a real way, had taken that freedom away. He resolved more than ever to continue his fight to put an end to the prejudice against Richard and his family.

He put a hand on Richard's shoulder. "What we have and need to foster for this town is respect for one another. After all, our differences are only skin deep."

Richard smiled. "At least I'm glad you realize that." After rolling his chew around in his mouth, Richard hacked and spat the tobacco juice. Dust jumped and covered the wad creating brown balls that rolled under his truck. After watching the tobacco juice roll under his truck, Richard wiped his mouth with the back of his hand.

Not approving of such a vile habit, Charles picked up his feet wincing at the sight of this display. However, Charles realized they were developing an important friendship, and Charles didn't want to do anything to sidetrack Richard. Moreover, he felt that Richard, more than anyone else, could give him advice about the letter that Jason wanted for the draft board.

Richard continued, as if paying no attention to Charles's reaction. "As for Jason, as far as I'm concerned, he saved my baby's life, and for that, I owe him a great debt that I don't quite know how I'll repay. At least, I don't want him to go to that damn war."

Charles sat in silence, not knowing what to say.

Richard continued. "So do me a favor, do something that gets him out of the war. Write the damn letter. I don't care what you put in it. Just write it down, and do it so the damn draft board will understand."

David Huffman

Charles stood and shook Richard's hand. "Thanks. Coming from you that means a lot." Remembering a comment he had heard Richard make in the co-op store several weeks ago, Charles said, "A dad's gotta do what a dad's gotta do. Talking with you about it makes it easier to do the right thing."

CHAPTER TWENTY-EIGHT

Charles wanted to spend time with Jason before he had to leave. He needed to learn more about his son. He had decided to write the letter, but what would he say, and how much would he place his reputation at risk? He knew that he couldn't tell any more lies. He agreed with Richard, he had to do everything he could to protect his son. Very proud of his son's actions, he had great hope that the long rift between them was over.

He found Jason in the kitchen, eating a piece of his mother's carrot cake. "I hope you've saved me a piece."

Mary smiled, and said, "Sure, here you go, Charles. I wouldn't let Jason eat it all and not save you a piece."

Charles turned to Jason. "You certainly shocked me. I never thought, not in a million years, that you had been there. I'm proud of you. What you did today, coming forward and telling what happened, took a lot of courage. I was scared the judge wouldn't believe you. Thank God, your prints were on the barrel, not on the handle of the gun. Anyway, I'm really proud of you for what you did, and most importantly, for coming forward and telling the truth."

"Thanks, Dad. I knew I had to come forward, just didn't quite know how to do it."

"You want to go fishing?"

"I'd love that."

They loaded the Jeep with fishing tackle and poles.

"We'll get some worms at Tom's place on the way to the lake. I delivered him a son this morning. I heard he has great night crawlers, just what the channel cats love. If that doesn't work, I have some great stink bait, which the fish will love."

Mary yelled after them, "Don't forget to take along some coffee and some of my fresh apple pie I baked this morning."

Jason helped Charles pull fishing line through the eyehooks on their rods. They put sinkers, fishing hooks, and bait in an old green fishing tackle box that had belonged to Charles's grandfather. "Been a long time, hope we can remember how to bait a hook. I thought we'd drive south to Smith's Lake and see if the catfish are biting. Haven't been there in years. Heard they have some great big channel cats feeding on the bottom of the lake."

"Sounds great."

They loaded the Jeep, got their afternoon snack and a thermos of coffee from Mary, and drove south of town to the lake. They parked on the road above the lake, and after grabbing their fishing gear, scrambled down to the water.

"Haven't fished for a long time. I wonder what they're biting on. Thought we'd try some stink bait first."

Jason turned his nose up. "Stink bait?"

"You bet. You'll get used to it."

Jason replied disgustedly, "If you say so, Dad."

Even though Charles hadn't tied a fishing line for some time, he remembered all the knots, and tied the hooks and sinkers with an alacrity that made it appear as if he did this every day. Planting his feet firmly, he grabbed the handle of the fishing pole. He reached back, and with a long arc, cast his line into the water. The sinker splashed into the center of the lake. Ripples spread in all directions as the line sank into the dark water. Securing his rod on a post, he turned his attention to help Jason set his line. That completed, he washed his hands in the lake water, poured himself a cup of coffee, and sat down to wait for a bite.

"Pour you a cup?"

"No, already had too much coffee for one day."

"Your mom packed some milk and apple pie."

They continued small talk about fishing. Charles kept hearing Mary's counsel. "Just relax and enjoy the day with your son." He wanted to confront Jason about the marijuana, and so many other things. As he looked out over the still water, he knew he must appear as calm as the lake and not overreact and drive his son away again.

Occasionally, a fish would jump. Charles said, "That's a big one, hope he takes my bait."

A meadowlark sang its familiar tune as it flew past them and into the briar patch on the south side of the lake. A lonely mourning dove cooed, complimenting the song of a

SUMMER SOLSTICE

Sandhill crane, as it fed in the shallows at the north end of the lake. A mallard, taking her morning bath, splashed in the water at the far end of the lake.

"C'mon, let's leave our poles and walk over to the dam. Remember how you used to love coming here and jumping off the diving board? Your mother and I worried whether the water was deep enough. Nothing bad happened, but nevertheless we worried."

"I didn't know you and Mom worried about me. Guess I never paid attention."

They walked along the dam to the south side of the lake. From this vantage point, they could see the water was high.

"We've had plenty of rain this spring, and more snow last winter than usual." Charles looked around nervously. "It's as full as I have seen it. I hope the rain stops, so we don't have another flood like we did in sixty-one."

He reached down and took a handful of dirt. Shaking his head, he said, "Nah, ground's too dry, not like it was the year of the flood. I think it'll be okay." His thoughts returned to fishing. "I wonder if they have stocked

David Huffman

the lake with fish this summer. Sure hope so. We'll have a better chance of taking back fish for supper."

Charles looked toward the Smokey Hill River, about three miles to the south. The lake drained water from the spillway into the river. Smoky Hill was barely visible, only six-feet wide at this point.

He motioned to a house in the valley between the dam and the river. "Alan called me. His kids had the croup and they couldn't breathe. After I took care of the kids, Alan asked me to stay for a meal. I stayed. It began to rain buckets. I couldn't see the road, and after trying to get up the hill, I had to turn back and spend the night with them. That night, the rain-washed out the roads and the phones went out. The Smoky Hill rose and started toward the lake. In the lightning, we could see the river eroding the hillside. We all thought the dam would h out and would flood Smithville and then us. I worried all night, and I was the happiest man alive when I found out the next day that you and Mary were okay."

"That's amazing, Dad, you were here in danger and all you could think about was our safety."

"Yes."

Jason smiled and put his arm around his dad. "Dad." Jason paused for several seconds. "I should have called. I came home because I didn't want to go to Nam and wanted you to help get me out of that. I realize now I had more on my mind. In a small way, I wanted to reconcile with you and Mom. I'm trying to make changes in my life, so you'll be proud of me."

"Son, I am proud of you, and even though you did the right thing to come forward, I don't particularly like the way you dress and your lifestyle, but I love you. All I want for you is to be successful in life."

"If I can get free of Vietnam, I want to go back to school. I want to be like you. Maybe I could even go to medical school. I've missed so much and I want to mend things."

"I've missed you, too." They hugged. "Sit down, Jason, and tell me about your life since you left."

Jason recounted the story of his journey over the past two years. He talked of marijuana and experimentation with LSD and how those were bad experiences.

Charles listened without comment or judgment even though he wanted to be critical. A part of Charles longed for the free spirit of his son. Was it too late for Charles? Perhaps he didn't have to be reckless to be a free spirit. Maybe he could learn something from his son to help himself more free.

Something, however, inside held him in check and told him to be careful. Jason is saying the right things, he thought, but he still wondered about Jason's motives. He wondered if he could really trust his prodigal son.

Charles said, "You'll have to go to college and make good grades. You'll have to be a little less rebellious, at least outwardly."

Jason nodded in agreement. They walked arm in arm back to their poles.

"You wait here," Charles said.

"Where're you going?"

"Since we didn't catch any fish, I'm going over to Alan's to call Mary and tell her we'll stop by the freezer downtown and get some steaks for dinner. We've got some celebrating to do."

They were both hungry and so they decided to pack up their gear and head back toward town.

Charles glanced in the rear-view mirror, watching the lake disappear as they climbed out of the ravine that held the lake and surrounding river delta. He tuned the radio to the Hays station to get the evening news. As they sped along the mesa, dust rose behind the Jeep, blocking the sun as it too raced into the horizon.

"Wish we could stay the night out here. It's going to be a beautiful night."

"Me too, Dad."

As they drove into town, the sun slipped behind the rain clouds that had formed in the west. Charles watched the combines and trucks rumble down the street. The harvest had begun.

"Life goes on," he said, barely audible.

Jason replied, "That it does."

They parked in front of the grocery store. Inside, they had a freezer box filled with packages of meat from the side of beef Charles had bought two weeks ago. Rummaging through the bin, Charles found three juicy porterhouse steaks.

After a sumptuous dinner, Jason said he was tired and he went to bed. Charles put his arm around Mary and guided her upstairs to their bedroom.

Charles pulled back the covers for Mary. She climbed into bed beside him, and snuggled into his arms. "Been a long and difficult weekend, Charles, I'm glad it's almost over. I wish Jason didn't have to leave in the morning. Have you thought about what you're going to do? Can you help him?"

Charles gave her a squeeze, and said he had talked with Richard about Vietnam. Struggling for the words, he told Mary he would write a letter for Jason. He told Mary the letter would document Jason's bad knees and ankles and argue that he should be 4F, and excuse him from the draft for medical reasons. At the very least, he hoped the letter would convince the medical examiner that Jason shouldn't be a foot soldier.

Mary listened intensely at Charles's plan. Then she said, "Couldn't you just put some X-rays of bad knees and feet with the letter?"

Charles sat up and looked Mary straight in the face. "I understand your motive. There's nothing more powerful than your love for our son and the desire to protect him. No mother would do differently. But to send false X-rays would be a lie."

He looked out the window. He thought about the irony of his comment to Mary, given his actions over the past weekend. Even though Charles wanted to do everything to help his son, he couldn't go further than the letter. The facts of the letter would be true, since Jason had injured his knees in a football game.

"I'm scared Charles. Hold me tight. Our baby is going tomorrow. I'm afraid they'll send him to that God forsaken place and he'll die.

"I know, honey." He held her tightly, not knowing how else to comfort her. One thing for sure, he would feel better after writing that letter for Jason, though he didn't have anyway of knowing whether the letter would change the recommendation of the physician, who would perform Jason's draft physical.

He took out a pen and paper, convinced that writing a letter to the draft board was the right thing, particularly after his talk with Richard. After all, Jason did have knees from playing football, and it wouldn't be a lie to write a letter pointing out Jason's problem.

CHAPTER TWENTY-NINE

Charles, Mary, and Jason were up early the next morning. After they ate a big breakfast, Mary packed Jason a lunch to take on the train. Even though the eastbound train wouldn't arrive until nine, they didn't want to be late, so they drove to the station and waited for the train.

Jason decided to forgo any further discussion about the letter. He got out of the car and walked to the track. Charles followed him.

"Dad, you remember when I used to walk to school every morning?"

"Yeah."

"I never told you, but when I got to these tracks, the train was always in our way. To get around it, I'd have to walk three blocks and miss the start of school. So, Max and I used to jump up on the flat car and climb over the train."

"Weren't you worried about getting caught, or that the train would start and you'd get crushed?"

"Nah, guess I thought we were invincible."

"I guess we all feel that way when we are young."

Charles reached in his coat pocket, pulled out an envelope, and handed it to Jason.

Jason looked at the envelope. "What's this?"

"It's a letter to the draft board and the medical examiner. Take it with you and give it to the doctors that examine you. I hope it helps."

Jason's eyes watered. "I don't know what to say."

"You don't have to say anything. I'm glad you're back. If you can fail the physical and get out of going to Vietnam, I hope you'll come home. I'd like to help you get back on your feet. Maybe you could go to college?"

"I'd like that. If I could get good grades and a medical degree, maybe I could come home and practice with you."

"I'd like that. I really would."

They walked arm in arm back to the car and waited. Just as the train was pulling into the station, Sandra drove up and got out of her car.

Sandra spoke with them. "The sheriff told me what happened. I must have been goofy from the blow on my head. I came out to say thanks and tell Jason goodbye."

Jason said, "You're welcome. What are you going to do?"

"I've decided to stay here and keep the pharmacy open. I've hired a student from the pharmacy school at the university. He will keep it open until he graduates, then maybe he'll take it over."

Jason replied, "Maybe I'll come back someday. I hope we can keep in touch."

Sandra smiled shyly. "I'd like that very much."

Charles, Mary, and Sandra watched Jason climb onto the train and walk back to a seat near the middle of the car. He opened the window and waved as the whistle blew, announcing the train was leaving the station.

Mary stayed along the side of the tracks while Charles and Sandra walked back to their cars.

"Doc, the sheriff told me that Joe had a brain tumor."

"Yes, Sandra, that's what I found when I did an autopsy."

"Do you think that's why he was so mean?"

"I don't know. Possibly. But I don't think anything can excuse him from what he did to you."

"Someday, somehow, I'll have to forgive him, so I can go on."

"Sandra, I overheard you saying you're going to keep the store open. I'm really glad. Ever think about opening a used-bookstore to sell mysteries?"

"Hadn't thought about that. You interested?"

"Yes, I am. I love mysteries."

CHAPTER THIRTY

Jason picked up his suitcase and boarded the morning train, nodding to the conductor as he gave him his ticket.

"Goin' to KC, young man?" The conductor punched Jason's ticket and handed the receipt back to him.

"Yeah."

He looked back at his parents, but they were engaged in a conversation with Sandra. Her presence both surprised and pleased him. Her hair sparkled in the morning sun. Less swollen, her face radiated with an aura, obscuring the remnants of her horrific abuse. He hoped she would take an interest in him, once he got through the draft.

The train, affectionately called the "milk train" had only one passenger car, in front of the caboose, and behind a long line of flatbeds, cattle cars, and oil tanks. Stopping in every town along the line, the train delivered the mail and food to towns on the prairie. The ride to KC would take all day, but that was okay with Jason; the longer the train ride, the longer he had to think about his future.

There were five other passengers on the train car. In the back, a young woman yelled at her two small children to keep them quiet. In the middle, a man snored loudly. Sprawled across the bench, his clothes disheveled, and his leathered face partially covered with a ten-gallon Stetson. Near the front of the railroad car, a little old lady sat quietly, knitting a pair of booties. Despite the early morning, the car was as hot as a baked potato.

The little lady asked, "Where ya going, sonny?"

"Kansas City."

Jason sat down across the aisle from her. "You?"

"I'm goin' to Salina to see my grandkids. Got a new granddaughter," she said with pride, holding up the baby booties.

Despite his smile and attempt to be accommodating, she seemed anxious as she looked over his hair and clothes. She slid closer to the window and away from Jason.

Jason stuck his head out the window and blew a kiss to his mom, yelling at the top of his lungs, "Thanks for everything." Then, specifically addressing his father, he said, "Thanks for the letter, Dad."

His mom waved back, then took a tissue from her pocket and wiped the tears from her face. His father also fumbled for a handkerchief, and blew his nose. Jason couldn't recall when he had seen his father cry. Despite their upcoming separation, he felt closer to his mom and dad than ever before. A long blast from the engine, followed by a head-jerking jolt, signaled that the nine o'clock Union Pacific pulling out of Smithville and heading east. He yelled goodbye at the top of his lungs, but the growing click-clack of the wheels on the train tracks drowned out his voice. The engine whistle blasted a warning to anyone in its path.

He watched the passing landscape. Two combines, one behind the other, moved gracefully along the well-groomed rows of ripe wheat. Six miles east of Smithville, the train sped, with a gush of wind, past a wheat silo.

The rhythm of the rail car lulled Jason to sleep.

David Huffman

******

His dream transported him back to Friday night.

As he dreamed, Jason began to hyperventilate. He heard Joe swearing at Sandra and pointing the gun at both of them.

Jason said, "My God, he's going to kill us. What'll I do? I can't let him kill us."

Jason reached out with his hands to grab the imaginary gun, and closed his fist.

"I've got the gun," he screamed.

Jason winced, feeling the searing heat of Joe's gun barrel. Jason recoiled from a blast of the gun that went off near his head.

"He missed me."

Sweating heavily, he struggled to overpower Joe. He heard the second shot. He saw Joe fall back. Jason let go of the gun. He felt Joe's hot blood splash on his cheek. As he wiped the blood from his mouth, he gawks at Joe's grotesque face.

"My God, I've shot him."

Jason dropped to his knees.

"I've killed him. I didn't mean to." Jason began to sob.

******

Gulping for air, and drenched with sweat, he grabbed the bar over the train seat in front of him and yelled at the top of his lungs.

The cowboy shook Jason's shoulder.

The little old lady said, "You all right, sonny?"

Jason sat back. Confused, he looked around at the concerned passengers. Everyone stared at him.

"You must've fallen asleep and had a bad nightmare," the old lady said, patting him on the shoulder. She took the cup of water from the younger woman, and handed it to Jason, saying, "There, there, you drink this, everything will be all right."

Jason, profusely sweating, took in a deep breath, and then drank the water. "Thanks." The dream had been so real. Had they heard the words he had spoken?

He thanked them, not wanting to tell them what had happened. Deep in his heart, he felt remorse for being a part of Joe's death, even though he knew in his head that he had done the right thing.

He sat quietly, absorbing the endless fields of wheat and the harvest. Up ahead, he heard a clanging of the crossing guard, signaling a passing train. As the train approached the bell, the sound grew louder and at a higher, more intense pitch. Then suddenly, as the other train passed, the sound of the bell diminished as the train sped toward the next little town on the prairie.

He thought about the sound. He knew about the Doppler Effect, and he thought about how this principle applied to his own life. Just like the clanging sound, as he got closer to people, his relationship with them grew more intense and stronger. However, as he pulled away, as he had done these past two years, the relationships with his family and friends faded into the background, just as the pitch of the bell dropped and faded into the distance.

One thing for sure, he wanted the louder, more intense relationships he had experienced during these past few days.

SUMMER SOLSTICE

Last Friday, when he drove into town, his only objective had been to get a letter from his dad, get out of the draft, and make sure Sandra was all right. He had done the right thing to save Sandra's life, even though it was hard. Moreover, he had done the right thing to come forward and tell the truth to the judge.

Jason thought about his friends. Max still had a ducktail and drove hot rods. None of his friends had had to go to Vietnam, because they were in college and that gave them a deferment. He wondered if the draft was truly a lottery. Somehow, he had to get beyond his friends and take responsibility for his life.

He took the envelopes out of his pocket, holding the draft notice in his left hand and his father's letter in his right. After opening the window for fresh air, he looked at the wheat fields and took a deep breath.

Jason understood that the wheat stalk supported the kernel. But, the kernel, the meat of the plant, provides the sustenance for life. He knew his family would be like the stock, and provide him support. To save his soul however, he knew he had to become like the kernel and be responsible for providing the sustenance for his own life.

"Is everything okay?" The elderly lady looked concerned.

He smiled. "Yes, everything's okay."

Slowly, intentionally, he put the envelope containing his draft notice in his pocket.

Purposely he tore up his father's letter, first in half, then in fourths, and then he hurled the pieces out of the window. With an overwhelming sense of happiness and satisfaction, he watched the pieces of the torn letter flutter in the hot wind, then disappear from view as the train sped toward his future.

ABOUT THE AUTHOR

David H. Huffman is a physician who was born, raised, and educated in Western Kansas. During his career, he received medical training in Baltimore at Johns Hopkins Hospital, taught at the University of Kansas, and practiced medical oncology in Colorado Springs, Colorado. During this time he published over fifty articles in scientific journals.

While he has published poems and short stories, this is his first novel. He and his wife Carol live in Colorado Springs.

Printed in the United Kingdom
by Lightning Source UK Ltd.
129939UK00001B/25-27/A

9 781403 351142